WITH LUKE, ELLA CAN SAY ANYTHING....

"Luke, can I ask you something?"

"Chipmunk to chipmunk?"

I smile, and he nods. "What makes you happy?"

"That's a tough one," he says. "Love, family . . . the usual." We walk for a few moments. "Why did that make you quiet?"

"Just thinking," I say, shifting my head to my other hand.

"Can I ask you something?"

"Chipmunk to chipmunk?"

He nods, then stops walking and faces me. "Why are you so sad?"

"Do you really want to know?" I ask, looking up at him. He nods, and I take another breath and tell him everything.

WITH ELLA, LUKE JUST NEEDS TO BE HIMSELF....

I think the most hopeful moment of my life was when we were in the Chip and Dale costumes, holding hands while we danced in a circle, and I could hear her laughing a little bit inside there, and I laughed just because she was, and I kept thinking, *We're in here . . . hidden, smaller than the thing around us, but still inside here.* If only your life were a costume, and you could just take it off when you wanted to.

I take another long look down the quiet walk that leads toward the castle, hoping I will see her, that she will know I'm out here and come find me. But as much as I want her to be, she's not there.

OTHER BOOKS YOU MAY ENJOY

DREAM

FACTORY

Brad Barkley

+

Heather Hepler

speak
An Imprint of Penguin Group (USA) Inc.

SPEAK
Published by the Penguin Group
Penguin Group (USA) Inc., 345 Hudson Street, New York, New York 10014, U.S.A.
Penguin Group (Canada), 90 Eglinton Avenue East, Suite 700,
Toronto, Ontario, Canada M4P 2Y3 (a division of Pearson Penguin Canada Inc.)
Penguin Books Ltd, 80 Strand, London WC2R 0RL, England
Penguin Ireland, 25 St Stephen's Green, Dublin 2, Ireland (a division of Penguin Books Ltd)
Penguin Group (Australia), 250 Camberwell Road, Camberwell, Victoria 3124, Australia
(a division of Pearson Australia Group Pty Ltd)
Penguin Books India Pvt Ltd, 11 Community Centre, Panchsheel Park, New Delhi - 110 017, India
Penguin Group (NZ), 67 Apollo Drive, Rosedale, North Shore 0632, New Zealand
(a division of Pearson New Zealand Ltd)
Penguin Books (South Africa) (Pty) Ltd, 24 Sturdee Avenue, Rosebank, Johannesburg 2196, South Africa

Registered Offices: Penguin Books Ltd, 80 Strand, London WC2R 0RL, England

First published in the United States of America by Dutton Books,
a division of Penguin Young Readers Group, 2007
Published by Speak, an imprint of Penguin Group (USA) Inc., 2009

1 3 5 7 9 10 8 6 4 2

CIP Data is available.

Speak ISBN 978-0-14-241298-5

Printed in the United States of America

For my mom and dad and especially for Terry.
Thank you for holding my hand on the tea cup ride.

—HEATHER

For Lucas and Alex, who still cross their fingers
when I play the claw machine.

—BRAD

Thank you to Stephanie Owens Lurie at Dutton
for always being so amazing. Our gratitude to Peter Steinberg at
Regal Literary for helping us find our way. Thank you to everyone
at Dutton and Penguin Young Readers for your continuing support and
kindness. Finally, thank you to Mom and Dad from Brad,
and to Harrison, Dan, and Bob from Heather.

DREAM FACTORY

Ella

I wasn't at all surprised when Cinderella gave me the finger.

They're supposed to stay behind the iron fencing separating the hotel from the monorail, but today there isn't any rent-a-cop blocking the way. "Just keep walking." I hear this murmured all around me, like some sort of mantra designed to carry us into the waiting train car and toward breakfast. "Don't they ever sleep?" Luke asks, pulling up even with me. "I mean, I saw that guy last night when I was coming back from the Electrical Parade." He points to a thin man leaning against the lamppost sipping from a Styrofoam cup.

"You mean Robin Hood?" I ask. Luke nods at me as he puts his hand up to block the sliding doors from closing. "He's *always* here," I say, stepping past him and onto the car.

"Do you see how he looks at Bryan?" he asks, lowering his voice.

"They all do that," I push damp hair out of my eyes. I still haven't acclimated to the heat. "It's as if each of us got our own worst enemy when we signed up for this."

"Maybe," he says, pulling back enough to let Jesse walk through. Jesse is big, linebacker big. The perfect Friar Tuck. "But that guy acts like it's personal, like *total* identity theft." I sit down on the bench just behind where Luke is standing so that I can watch the crowd through the open door.

We know who they are by the signs they're carrying. Buzz Lightyear's simply has the words TO 401K AND BEYOND, which I think lacks creativity. Cinderella is busy talking on her cell phone. Her sign, which she has propped against the fence, reads MICKEY CAN KISS MY GLASS (SLIPPER). Captain Hook's features the Jolly Roger with a mouse head where the skull is supposed to be. I'm pretty sure he's the one that actually starts things.

I hear a thud against one of the windows near the back of the train car. One long *Ewww* is followed by another thud, then another. "What . . ." I begin, but I don't finish my question. Amy comes in with a yellow streak on her face.

"Hurry!" Luke yells at the last few people now running for the tram. There are several more eggy thuds against the windows as Bryan and some guy with blond hair lunge through the door. Luke lets the door slide shut, and we listen to more thuds as we wait for the autopilot to respond to the door sensors. I stare out the window at the crowd slowly turning back toward the parking lot. I imagine that they will have to prepare for the next monorail, which will be by in about fifteen minutes to take people to the main gate staging area. We pull away from our hotel, which has been converted into a dorm for now. They even took away the king-size beds so they could fit a couple of crappy twin beds in each room. They got rid of the phones in our rooms and installed the crappy PA system with wires running everywhere, so they can make announcements and try to keep us in line. Just when I'm thinking about how crammed in we are, someone sits down next to me on the bench. It's the blond guy who jumped on with Bryan.

"You're Ella, right?" he asks, pulling at the bottom of his T-shirt. I nod as he makes a pocket with his shirt to catch the mess slowly sliding down his front. "You don't know what gets out raw eggs, do you?" he says. I shake my head before turning to stare out the window again. "This isn't quite what I imagined," he says, and I look over at him again, slowly this time, but he doesn't seem to notice.

"Not really the Happiest Place on Earth, is it?" I say, staring back out the window.

"Just not right now," he says, trying to bundle his shirt with his hand.

"Just wait until breakfast." I look over at Luke, who's sitting across the car, willing him to look at me so that I can give him the get-me-out-of-here look, but he's laughing at something Cassie said. The guy beside me uses his sleeve to wipe at the streaks of yellow slowly making their way down his cheek.

"Breakfast is bad?" the blond guys says.

I shrug. "It's mostly just posing for pictures. That and answering questions."

"Like what?"

"Mostly the usual. 'What time's the parade?' 'Where can we rent strollers?' That's the parents. It's the kids you have to watch out for."

"Why?"

"They want the *dirt*. Like, 'Does Captain Hook really have a hook for a hand?' 'How can Ariel hold her breath for so long?' 'Do you really have a fairy godmother?'"

"Do you?"

"Not that I know of," I say. "I mean, if I do, she's keeping a really low profile." I look past him to where Amy is making bug eyes at me. *"He's cute,"* she mouths at me. I squint at her, which makes her smile.

"So, Ella," he says, "I guess we're going to be spending a lot of time together."

"Why's that?" I ask. I'm trying not to be rude, but I'm really not into the whole Disney Family thing that they keep talking about around here. After only a week I started to question my decision to come here, but going home early is out of the question. All this cheerful friendliness is starting to take its toll on me.

"I thought you knew," he says. He folds the end of his shirt over onto itself, making a larger pocket. "James pulled his hamstring last night when he ran after you on the stairs." I raise my eyebrows. I hadn't seen James after the parade, but I thought maybe he'd just turned in early.

"So, you—"

"I went from ice-cream scooper to prince in one night."

"That is quite a promotion," I say. Amy is waggling her eyebrows up and down so fast that I can almost feel the breeze from where I am sitting.

"So, Ella, what do you think?" he asks. I think Amy's eyes are going to roll out of her head if she doesn't stop looking at me that way. "You think I have what it takes to be Prince Charming?"

I shrug, realizing that really isn't the answer that he's hoping for. Even on my good days I'm not that into the whole flirty thing. And today, with the heat and the smell of rotten eggs and the fact that I am going to have to break in the fourth Prince Charming in a month, I'm definitely not feeling like playful banter with someone. Even if that someone has crinkly brown eyes and curly blond hair. "Sure," I finally manage. "I'm sure you'll do fine."

"You're telling me you never made the connection?" Luke says to me out of the corner of his mouth. Mr. William "Call me Bill" Tubbs is at the front of the room giving us his daily pep talk. Today it's peppered with lots of talk about unity and the Disney Family, which rings kind of false considering that any day they could settle the strike and all of us would be sent home with a set of souvenir mouse ears and a free parking coupon. "How is that possible?" Luke asks. He leans back in his chair, propping up his feet on the head of his costume, which rests in front of him.

"Do you even know how much that would freak some little kid out if they could see you now?" I whisper.

"Stop changing the subject," Luke says. "You never thought—Ella. Cinder . . . ella."

Mr. Tubbs taps the map that is projected on the back wall, saying something about important visitors from the media.

"Why would I? My real name is Eleanor."

Luke chokes on his coffee. "Eleanor?"

"It gets worse," I whisper.

"How much worse could it be?"

"Gertrude."

"Man, that's bad." Luke shakes his head as if I just told him I have a terminal disease. I elbow him hard, but he barely feels it through the thick fur of his costume.

"Now you," I say.

"Oh no," he says, holding up one paw. "I don't tell anyone my middle name."

"Worse than Gertrude?"

Mr. Tubbs clears his throat, making me look back at the front of the room. "Mickey will be at breakfast today." Mr. Tubbs taps a stack of papers on the table as he talks, lining up the edges. "Please take a copy of the schedule and try to be on time, people. Yesterday we had a fiasco at the Tea Party."

"A tea party fiasco," I whisper. Luke laughs too loudly, making Mr. Tubbs look over at us.

"So," Amy asks later, as she helps me to pin my hair up under my wig. "Who is he?"

"Who?" I ask, working my fingers into my gloves. I've been going through an average of four pairs a day. Amusement parks aren't really built for the white-glove treatment.

"The guy on the train."

"You are not going to believe this," I say, turning to check the back of my dress. Two days ago I went a whole hour with my skirt tucked into the top of my tights until one of the Merry Men told me. "He's the new Prince Charming."

"What happened to James?" Amy asks, twisting her hair up into a ponytail.

"Pulled hamstring."

"Man, how many is that? Three?"

"Four." I help Amy tug her wig down over the back of her head and adjust the headband to keep it from falling forward.

"I keep forgetting the Puker," she says, laughing.

"Yeah, who eats sushi at an amusement park?"

"At least this one's cute," she says, fluffing out her sleeves. Last week they made her carry this silk bluebird on her shoulder until a little girl got hysterical because she thought Snow White was into taxidermy.

"I don't care what he looks like. I am so done with princes."

"At least you *get* one," Amy says, taking my hand and leading me toward the doors. "I get a third of a prince. I have to share mine with Ariel and Belle."

"I thought Belle was with the Beast." I can hear the murmuring of the crowds as the first group of characters makes its way through the doors and toward the tables.

"Ella, he isn't always the Beast. Sometimes he's the charming prince."

"What's the difference between the charming prince and Prince Charming?"

"Your guy's *name* is Prince Charming," she says, giving my arm a squeeze. "Capital *P* capital *C*. He's the real deal." We pause to allow Donald and Daisy Duck to have their own entry. "You ready?" Amy asks, giving me her best if-I-smile-any-bigger-my-face-is-going-to-split-in-two smile. We walk through the doorway and into the brightly lit restaurant, where dozens of families await. They have saved and planned and traveled and gotten up early just to meet us. To take pictures of us that will end up in a scrapbook or a photo album or a shoe box so that someday someone will take it out and say, *Hey look, there I am with Cinderella. That was the last time we went on a vacation before our parents got divorced or Mom died of cancer or Bobby ran away.* I smile at the family sitting in the first booth that I come to. Two little girls sit in between their parents. They have matching T-shirts with swirls of pearlized ribbons and sprays of flowers, surrounding the words DISNEY PRINCESSES.

"Look who it is," the mom says a little too shrilly. I have gotten used to this in the few weeks that I've been here. The too-big smiles. The too-loud laughs. The manic looks on everyone's faces. The girls just stare at me with huge eyes, as if at any moment I might jump across the table and gobble them up. "It's Cinderella," the mom says, her voice hitting an octave nearly too high for human hearing. The little girls are frozen, pressed together at the back of the curving booth. I start to move on to the next table, where Goofy is entertaining a family by juggling a couple of apples and the pepper shaker, but the mom isn't done with me yet. "Don't you girls want a picture with Cinderella?" she asks, pulling the arm of the girl closest to her. I bend down, thinking that maybe if I make myself smaller, they won't be so afraid. Slowly they slide out of the booth and make their way over to stand with me.

"Smile," the dad says, waving his hand in an effort to make them step closer to me. His voice is brittle and tired. I smile as he clicks off one, then two, then three shots, turning the camera slightly with each one. The mom is pushing at her cheeks, exaggerating her own smile into something that barely resembles anything remotely happy. I look down at the girls standing quietly beside me. The older one has her arm around her little sister, who is trying to smile despite the fact that her cheeks are wet with tears.

· · ·

Normally, I would have had to go through several auditions to even get a shot at being one of the fur characters, but I got Cinderella just by showing up. Management was desperate. They had sold-out Princess breakfasts, waiting lists for the Chip and Dale campfires, not to mention the thousands of people who just come to the park and mill around, cameras at the ready to "make a memory that will last a lifetime." The union gave management until Memorial Day to meet their demands. Better work conditions, free meals, cleaner costumes, a dental plan. I took the bus to Orlando when I heard the radio ad announcing immediate open auditions for all characters.

The real reason I got the part wasn't because my hair was the right color (it's brown, not blond,) or because I could sing (not even "Happy Birthday" or "Jingle Bells") or because I had a great audition (I tripped on my gown on the way into the room), but because I was the right size. Of the nearly two dozen other girls who showed up for the audition, I was the only one who fit into the costume without any alterations. Thinking that they were casting us for a day or two tops, keeping wardrobe changes to a minimum was a priority.

I have to admit Cinderella is a pretty plum role. Most of my day is spent hosting various meals around the resort. There's the character breakfast every morning after our real breakfast, then the Cinderella brunch at the castle, then the Princess Tea Party. In between times I have to stage the whole running-down-the-castle-steps-and-losing-my-glass-slipper thing. I get married every afternoon at three, and then I have a break until the Electrical Parade at nine. Luckily, there's another Cinderella who does all the shows. Almost every face character has a duplicate in the performance area. Those people are the dancers and singers. Mostly all we do is smile and wave and sign autographs for people. The only thing that keeps tripping me up is the voice. Stacy, the princess handler, is in charge of making sure that we all stay in character when we're working. She keeps telling us that we have to talk more properly. "Think vaguely British." So in addition to trying not to break my neck running down stairs in heels and trying not to sweat more than a princess should, I walk around telling people that I *shan't* be at Aurora's buffet, that I *simply cawn't* believe this heat, and that I would *rawther* have a glass of water than juice. That's the other thing. Even though I go to about seven meals a day, I'm usually starving come dinnertime. Stacy made it very clear on the first day: Princesses don't eat.

I have to change into my brunch gown before heading over to the castle. "Need help?" Amy asks, stepping into the changing room. I turn and let her pull at my zipper. After the skirt-in-stocking incident last week, I've taken to wearing shorts under my gowns. Around us, girls are suiting up for the day. Jessie from *Toy Story* leans toward the mirror, using a brown eyebrow pencil to give herself freckles.

"How sweet would that be?" I ask, nodding in her direction. "Jeans."

"I may never wear a dress again," Amy says, pulling at her bodice. "It could be worse though."

I step out of my blue gown and hang it back up on the rack. "How's that?" I take my pink dress, my hanging-around-the-castle dress, from the hanger and begin pulling it on. "I mean, besides the animals," I say, watching as Winnie the Pooh adjusts her head in the mirror.

"What about Julie?" she says, nodding over my shoulder to where a girl with long red hair is adjusting her seashell bikini top. "Or even Devin?"

"I agree that sitting around in the stinking grotto all day with your legs jammed into a plastic fish tail while prepubescent boys try to cop a feel through your shells would suck, but how is Princess Jasmine any worse off than us? I mean, at least she gets to wear pants."

"Yeah. *See-through* pants. That and a tiny halter top. Can you say five hundred crunches a day?"

"True. Not to mention that jerk who plays Aladdin. What's his name?"

"You just don't like him because he got you in trouble."

"I still can't believe he told on me for that."

"Ella, you told a little girl that you hated the color pink."

"Well, I do."

"So not the point," Amy says, but I can tell she's having a hard time keeping her smile in check. "You do, of course, understand that the color pink is nearly synonymous with the Princesses, don't you?"

"Well, duh," I say, spreading the skirt of my dress wide. That does it. We stand there grinning at each other for a moment before Stacy claps her hands and tells us that we need to get a move on. "See you this afternoon," I say, picking up my parasol (pink to match my dress).

Amy waves at me with the back of her fingers as she hurries out the door toward the Haunted Forest. I follow more slowly. The castle's less than a quarter mile from anywhere in the park. There, I know, little girls are eating star-shaped peanut butter and jelly sandwiches and drinking apple juice out of teacups while they wait for me to arrive. For sixty dollars each, they get brunch, a souvenir photo, a Cinderella doll, and their own golden crown.

It's hot outside, and the park is starting to fill up. I walk past the shrubs trimmed to resemble Mickey and Donald and Goofy. Two little girls pick at a cloud of blue cotton candy. Their blue lips frame blue teeth as they smile at me. A boy with a green baseball cap sticks his tongue out at me, purple from his snow cone. A family cuts in front of me, and I have to stop short to avoid running into them. Mom is pushing a double stroller filled with two kids, a backpack, two animal-shaped sippy cups, an umbrella, and something blue and green and shiny. Dad keeps folding and refolding a map, trying to make it go back to its original shape. He is following his wife so closely that he keeps stepping on the back of her flip-flops and hitting her in the back of the head with the edges of the map.

It's because the little boy is trailing behind them and doesn't look at me that I notice him. In one hand he holds a giraffe by its neck, its head bent at an impossible angle from too many games of hide-and-seek, too many nights snuggling under the covers, and too many times crammed into carts at the grocery store. His other hand is clutching the ribbon attached to a Mickey Mouse balloon. It's one of the double balloons, a blue mouse head inside a clear bubble. Mom stops the stroller and grabs the map from Dad.

I pause by the waterfall and watch as the boy pulls on the ribbon, making Mickey's face dip toward him and then bounce back up into the air. Mom and Dad are moving again, but the little boy stays where he is, eyes glued on the balloon. He doesn't move from his spot even when a woman nearly hits him with her shopping bag brimming with mouse ears and Tinker Bell wands. Whether it is the jostling crowd or the tug of his father's hand, suddenly the balloon bounces up much higher than before, but this time there isn't anything to stop its ascent.

"My balloon," he says, much more softly than I would have imagined.

"I told you to hang onto it," his father says, pulling him forward.

"I did," I hear him say as he is pulled past me.

"Not tightly enough."

The balloon dips twice in the air before it catches a fast moving air current and sails off over the lagoon. It grows smaller and smaller in the sky until I can't see it at all anymore. The cobblestones are tricky to navigate, especially in high heels. Especially when you're late. You have to watch where you place each foot to avoid falling, but instead of watching the road in front of me like I should, I keep finding myself staring up at the sky.

Luke

"Luke, we have some costuming issues," Mr. Forrester says to me, tapping his wedding ring on his chair. "Your name has come up."

I nod at him, twitching my foot so that the loose string on my Chucks makes its own *tap-tap* against the floor beneath his desk. On top of the desk, there's a framed picture, like you'd expect, but instead of wife and kids, it's just him, in a suit, smiling while he receives a gold statuette shaped like Mickey Mouse. Beside the photo is a desk calendar, "Daily Affirmations for Corporate Survival." I'm not sure I understand what that means. Today's affirmation is "A Knowing Smile Is Your Best Weapon." Mr. For rester also has a Mickey Mouse–shaped pencil sharpener, ashtray, wastebasket, and Oriental rug. The ashtray has a cigar butt resting on Mickey's ear. The phone on his desk, like those of all the management people here, is an actual plastic statue of Mickey Mouse holding the receiver in his white-gloved hand. I imagine Mr. Forrester shouting into that phone, maybe firing someone, while Mickey covers his ears and asks why everyone can't just be friends. Then again, it might be *me* who's about to get fired, so suddenly the whole idea is not so funny. I keep watching my hands, cracking my knuckles, still surprised some days to look down and see actual human fingers instead of fur-covered paws.

Mr. Forrester adjusts his tie clip and purses his lips. "Luke," he says, "I want you to imagine I'm a six-year-old boy. A towheaded youngster who has come with Mom and Dad to the happiest place on earth. Are you with me?"

"What does towheaded mean?" I say, just to mess with him. "Is that like a birth defect?"

"No, Luke, it means blond. Blond hair. With me?"

"Yes, sir," I tell him, playing along, and then suddenly I *do* see it, Mr. Forrester in an OshKosh jumper with kangaroos on the pockets, except he still has his silk tie and his wingtip shoes. He's polishing the toe of one of those shoes right now with his fingers. My dad has the same kind of shoes, a pair in brown and a pair in black. I will never figure out why somebody thought a pattern of swirly holes was a good look. And it's weird. My brother graduated college and went to work for Dad at the drilling company, and now he has those same shoes. It's like wingtip shoes are your ticket into adulthood, or maybe the big secret is that your college diploma is really just a gift certificate for Pic 'N Pay Shoes, and you redeem it the next day. For girls, maybe it's those bulky, serious-looking suits with the shoulder pads, or maybe some kind of hair. I don't know. All I know is, I don't ever want those shoes.

Mr. Forrester looks to the ceiling now as he talks. "I'm a six-year-old boy proudly wearing my mouse ears with my name stitched on the front. Let's say Jimmy, for argument's sake."

"I was thinking Reggie," I say. He gives me a knowing smile, just like the calendar says to.

"Okay then, Luke. That's fine. Little Reggie is walking along happy as can be, and then happens upon what scene? Do you see where I'm going with this? He sees Dale—with Chip nowhere around—sprawled on the ground, presumably dead, and as if that weren't enough, our little cartoon friend is *decapitated*, his head beside him." He picks up a paper clip and tosses it into the plastic coffee cup on his desk. "Luke, we could be talking about a lifelong trauma."

I take a deep breath. "Mr. Forrester, it was ninety-seven degrees that day; I had just done a parade. I was hot. I took off the head and stretched out in the shade. It was five minutes."

"Three reports," he says, then picks up the reports and tosses them back down. "Lifeless chipmunk body, head in the grass. Then what? You let your head roll down the grassy knoll. One mother screamed. We could be sued. It's my job."

His job, despite the big-deal office and all the Mickey crap, was pretty low on the totem pole, everyone said. He was officially the Fur Character Coach, in charge of anyone inside the park who has to wear a head—Goofy, Donald, Daisy, Winnie the Pooh—all the fur characters. Of course, with the heat and claustrophobia it's the worst job in the park unless you count cleaning toilets, and for corporate climbers fur coach is the worst job in management. Everyone knows Mr. Forrester wants to work his way up to Princess Handler, which actually seems like a disturbing job title for a middle-aged man.

"What if I faint?" I ask him. "What if I don't take a break, and I just faint? Wouldn't *that* be a lot worse for you to see, assuming you're a six-year-old girl?"

"Boy."

"A six-year-old boy?"

While he thinks about this he picks up the cold cigar butt and taps it against Mickey's nose. Every time I see anything Mickey, I can't help singing that song inside my head. *M-I-C . . . See you later.* That's what I would like to say right now to Mr. Forrester. He shows me the cigar butt before throwing it into the trash. "Don't ever start," he says. "They killed my dad."

"I won't."

He nods. "You have to suck it up, Luke," he says. "You're *Dale*, for godsakes. A household name. Show a little pride."

Actually, if being a fur character is the worst job in the

park, then being Dale has to be the worst job among the fur characters. When I got the gig and told my mom and dad and brother, all of them were like, *"Who?"* And I mean, it makes sense. Someone out of the blue says, "I play Dale," then that would be the question to ask, and I always, always have to say, "You know, as in Chip and?" Say Goofy, say Donald, it's automatic. Dale is not automatic. Ashtray Mickey has two black eyes from the cigar butt, like he's been in a fight. I nod at Mr. Forrester. Really, if I lose this job, then I have to temp at my dad's office again, like I did last summer, and somehow that striped necktie makes me suffocate worse in the AC than the fur head does in the heat. When I got this job, my dad told me one of his "wise stories" about how one summer he had a job driving an ice-cream truck, selling Good Humor bars. The next summer he was off to N.C. State. He tells the story and then tells me to go ahead, get it out of my system, and sometimes when I'm inside the costume, down inside the fur and plastic and latex looking out through the mesh, hearing my own breath, breathing my own sweat, watching my paws shake hands with some kid for the five-hundredth time that day, I think, At least I'm someone else, at least I can stay in here, hidden, where my dad can't find me, where the drilling company can't find me, where the wingtip shoes can't find me. I'm the only one who knows I'm in here, and maybe I never have to come out, never have to get myself out of my system. I tell Mr. Forrester that being Dale is my vocation, my calling, my mission in life. I tell him I want to make memories that last a lifetime. I put my heart into it, the way I do when I'm talking to Dad or the principal at school, and I can tell he believes it. In his job he has to believe it. I'm pretty good. So good that, for half a second, even I believe it.

Sometimes I talk to the Dale head. I creep myself out doing it, like I'm going to turn into one of those ventriloquists in the movies who sits by while his dummy commits murders, and the whole time you know it's him, not the dummy, since he's crazy as hell. But I don't want to kill anyone, and during breaks, the Dale head is just sitting there grinning at me like I can do no wrong, and so I talk to it. I mean, who else? That jerkwad they hired to play Prince Charming? Prince Dumb-ass, maybe. I mean, this guy is *not* smart, too much chlorine in the gene pool. The other day at breakfast he said he's not supposed to eat Grape-Nuts cereal because he's allergic to nuts. I don't even know the guy's name, only that since he came, he is always hanging around Ella. *Always.* That, and he looks like one of the Hardy Boys.

And as for the hitting on Ella part, I don't like that. I look down at Dale's head and say so.

"Dale, I don't like that," I tell him, because right now Biff or Kip or Whoever is following after her, again, touching the satin ribbon that's gathered at the small of her back, and then she runs off and he chases after her, running so hard his epaulets are bouncing.

. . .

"His epaulets are bouncing," I say to Dale, only because I like saying it. Dale keeps grinning at me from his side of the bench, wide-eyed. His personality is pretty one-dimensional. He will never understand her, I tell Dale. Not ever. I bet they could be married for like ten years, and he would never even make her laugh unless he slipped on a banana peel or something.

"Talking to your own head again?" I look up, and Cassie is drinking a bottle of water, standing over me.

"It's my hobby," I say to her. She sits down in front of one of the five fans that are always blowing in the break tent and rubs the dripping bottle across her forehead.

"Yeah, I wonder what Freud would have to say about that." She takes a long swallow and sets her own head down on the grass between her feet.

"Sometimes a disembodied chipmunk head is only—"

"Okay, Luke. You know Mr. Forrester told us to take our breaks together. We're supposed to be Chip *and* Dale, not Chip *or* Dale." She pours some of the water over her head and lets it drip off the end of her blond ponytail. She plays lacrosse and is in better shape than anyone I've ever met. I think she takes her breaks not because she wants to but because she's supposed to.

"Sorry, Cass," I tell her, reaching out to hold her hand. And I am sorry. We have kinda-sorta been dating the last three weeks. My mom would call her a "great catch," the way she sometimes does, as if girls are fish, or maybe line drives over the centerfield wall. And I know she is . . . pretty, blond, sexy, athletic, smart. She is on her way to Brown in the fall, to major in prelaw and women's studies and French. I didn't even know there was such a thing as a triple major. When she got the letter about her scholarship, she ran around all excited, and everyone congratulated her, and I kissed her, then wondered out loud if Brown was the only university in the country named for a color. I really did wonder, like, is there a White? Gray? That sounds pretty likely, actually. Black? I don't think so. Then she got mad at me for saying it, and I didn't even understand what she was mad at. I really do like her. I like walking around the park with her at night, holding hands. I like kissing her. Except I always wonder if it just feels like I like her in the way I'm supposed to, or maybe *because* I'm supposed to. How do you know when you *really* like someone? Or love someone?

Cass stands behind me and pours water over my head, the icy finger of it running down my spine; then she leans over, tips my head back, and kisses me, another finger down the spine. She can kiss, for sure, but once we ended up making out in the costumes, and that was just a little too weird. Even for me. At least we took off the heads.

"Secret party Saturday, basement of the dorm," she says. "We're in charge of music. I suggested a costume party, but that idea didn't go over too well." She gives my hair a little tug with her fingers. "That was a joke, sweetie."

I nod, trying to tune in to what she's saying, but instead, I'm watching Prince Moron, who is right now in one of the other break tents with Ella, pretending *again* that he doesn't understand their waltz steps, just so he has an excuse to put his hands on her.

"Sam?" Cass says.

I look back at her. "Nope."

"Not some variation? Samuel? Samson?"

"Not even close. So cold you're freezing."

"I wish. Tell me."

"Never." I blow on my hands, still trying to cool off. Break is over in five minutes. Sometimes I just can't face going back out there, dancing another dance, shaking another five-year-old hand, hearing some redneck with a mullet make another joke about the Chippendale dancers.

"Stuart," Cass says.

"You said that yesterday." She is obsessed with figuring out my middle name, which I will never, *never* tell anyone. Make me do the Acorn Dance in the Sahara for ten busloads of ADD-afflicted second graders during a Ritalin shortage, and still I won't tell. No one, ever. Luke S. Krause is my full and given name. The End.

"Slappy," Cass says, and kisses me again.

"Ooh, so close," I tell her, cupping her face. Across her shoulder, in the other tent, the Hardy Boy Prince is showing Ella how he can fill his mouth with gas from his butane lighter, then make a flame shoot out. His lone "bad boy" trick, and he doesn't even smoke. He did it at breakfast right after the big Grape-Nuts scare, and everyone applauded while I sat there hoping for some tragedy the coroner would later term "cranial explosion." No such luck.

"I don't know why he bothers you," Cass says, following my gaze over to them.

"Who?"

Cassie smirks. "They probably deserve each other. She's so weird. I mean, just the other day I saw her standing out in front of the castle, and she's just standing there, like she's all sad, looking up into the sky. That's pretty strange, Luke."

I nod, looking up at Cass's perfect white teeth, her blue eyes. I guess that's why it bothers me so much. Ella *is* kind of strange, a round peg plunked down in the middle of the square old world, and I know that doofus is about a million years away from ever getting her. So it's just sympathy, I'm thinking. Or empathy . . . I forget the difference. Like once I read in some gardening article that if you put a watermelon blossom inside a plastic milk jug, then you can grow a square watermelon. I feel sorry for the watermelon. Yesterday I asked Cass—when they finally let us out of here—to go with me out to this place called Shell Island. When the tide washes out there at dusk, all these huge tidal pools are left behind, and they're filled with starfish, anemones, urchins, barnacles, crabs . . . everything, and I can spend two hours just watching, until it's too dark to look. When I asked her to go, there was a long and puzzled look, and then her face brightened. "Can we get beer?" she asked.

I don't know how to explain why beer ruins the idea of seeing the tide pools. I just know it does.

Break is over, and we put our heads back on. Cass rubs our vinyl noses together, then mimes putting her paws over her heart. She does this sometimes during the parade, and twice Mr. Forrester has called us in to remind us that Chip and Dale are not gay. We high-five each other and make our exaggerated stroll back out onto the streets of the park, holding paws. Paw-holding is okay. Cass is carrying a large Styrofoam acorn in her other hand. I feel hidden, not just inside the suit but inside myself, hidden in a way that makes the heat tolerable, makes Mr. Forrester tolerable. Hidden in plain sight, which has been my strategy for surviving family and school and just about everything else. Maybe life in the suit is like life in the tide pools . . . the world of yourself is both large and small, and that bigger world is just some idea of an ocean, something deep and dark you struggle to recall.

"We're on, Slappy," Cass says, and the show begins.

That night after the fireworks and late dinner in the dorm and too much coffee for me, I can't sleep. We aren't supposed to leave the dorm after lights-out, but most of us do all the time, anyway. The chaperones have their own little apartments, and they are clueless. I walk outside a little after one in the morning, according to the clock tower, and it's the only time I can really say I like the park. There is enough of a breeze to cool things off a little, and I like the emptiness, like how it feels. Like maybe way back someone believed this place really would seem magical, full of wonder . . . all the crap you hear around this place every day, but everywhere else only at Christmas. Maybe they thought it would seem like another world, set apart from the real one, instead of just the real world on hyperdrive—more selling, more money, more worn-out families, more hype. Like Dr. Frankenstein thinking he's creating life—before the monster started killing. The romance of not knowing anything. As I'm thinking all of this, moving toward the castle, the silhouette of someone sitting on one of the benches takes shape from out of the dark, and then that someone turns into Ella, arms around her knees, gently rocking back and forth.

"Hey, you," I say.

She nods. "Luke, how was it today?"

"Same. You?"

"Mostly the same. A radical feminist fifth-grader wanted to know if I wasn't reinforcing negative female stereotypes with my dependence on Prince Charming."

I laugh and sit beside her, kicking off my flip-flops. "How'd you explain that one?"

"I think I said something along the lines of 'get away from me.' It seemed to satisfy her curiosity."

"Well, it's a good answer. It has layers."

"Thank you. I thought so, too."

"So are you?" I step on the back of one of the flip-flops, so it tilts upward.

She frowns. "Am I what?"

"Starting to depend on Prince Charming. He's around you all the time," I say with more force than I'd meant.

"Um, that's kinda how the story goes? Anyway, he's cute, I'm told."

"You don't buy it?"

She slaps a mosquito on her shin. "Yeah, I guess so. How's the girlfriend?"

I shrug. "She's fine."

She leans forward, and I look at her. "It's weird. This place feels haunted at night," she says, "but it's like reverse haunted."

I think about that one. "Reverse haunted?"

She nods. "Yeah, like when it's empty and quiet, all the life flows back into it. Haunted by life. The death is all the noise and chaos during that day. Does that make sense?"

I nod. "I was just thinking that, something like that. It seems almost hopeful at night, you know? Like it'd be a great place to visit if no one was here."

She nods again, as if she's just found the one other person who speaks her language. "Yes, exactly. You mix every color together, you get black. Daytime here is every color."

"You should have this conversation with Prince Charming. He can do more tricks with his lighter."

"You know," she says, "you have the saddest eyes I have ever seen."

For a moment I can't breathe. "Is that bad?"

"I don't know, Luke. You're in there, not me. Is it?"

"Let me ask you a question. If you went to the beach, and it was dusk, and you were looking in the tide pools, and you just sat there watching all the life swim around in there, what would be your beverage of choice for such an outing?"

She doesn't hesitate. "Hot chocolate."

"Why?"

"Because it would be cool outside because it's late fall, and because this particular tide pool is in New England somewhere, on a rocky beach instead of a sandy one, and you have to wear fleece jackets, and the wind whips your hair around, and you sit on a blanket to watch the tide pools, watch the sun sink lower until the cold is trying to push you inside, and right then, Luke S. Krause, you are going to thank me for bringing that thermos of hot chocolate." She smiles, but it's a smile like she is far away from here.

I nod, and the clock on the tower edges toward two. "Good answer," I say. "You're just full of them, aren't you?"

"Well, I do what I can." She looks up at me again. And just then I think that her face is reverse haunted, too . . . when she smiles, there is a sadness to match whatever it is she sees in my eyes.

3

Ella

My parents lost it when Ash died. Some people thought it was because it happened so close to the holidays. The Christmas tree blinking while the trooper talked with my father. The scent of balsam fir forever the smell of grief. There were those who decided it was because he was the firstborn, the son, that they took it so hard. Named for our grandfather. The spitting image of our father. I thought it was something else. I thought it was because there was no cause to join, no petition to sign, no law to support, no one to blame. I thought it was because no matter how many hours you spent thinking about it, no matter how many ways you tried to get your head and your heart around it, there was no way to explain why it happened. What happened—that was easy. An icy road. A dark December night. Ash was probably tired. His first semester of college was behind him. Finals were over, and he was anxious to get home. A duffel bag full of dirty laundry was found in a creek bed alongside the road. Three packages wrapped in the same shiny green foil were found in the snow. A Styrofoam cup, stained brown from coffee, was still wedged in the cupholder.

"We just didn't expect to get an assignment so soon," my mother said, the day they decided to go. "It's only for a few months." She pulled at the zippers on my duffel bag. We were all taking off in different directions, leaving the empty house behind us.

"Six," I said, tracing the initials on my suitcase. HRM, not mine. I bought it at the L.L. Bean outlet, left by someone who changed his mind.

"It's not forever, Ella. And you'll be in school before you know it." The letter from Vermont College lay folded in the bottom of my backpack. "Meanwhile, you'll have an adventure," she said, already turning away from me to walk down the hall toward the kitchen. "Who wouldn't want to live in Florida during the winter?"

"I think I figured out slugs." I take another bite of watermelon. Plain, not the one doused in vodka that everyone else seems to be eating. I lean back against the brick wall, letting the juice drip onto the concrete between my feet.

"You mean their psychology?" Luke asks, biting his own wedge of watermelon, also plain.

"No, I mean why they exist." I find myself saying strange things to Luke, things I would never say to anyone else. The thing is, he seems to get it. To get *me*. The music thumps behind us, making the sliding glass doors that lead into the basement vibrate. Everyone else is inside, hunched around the folding table, bouncing quarters into a glass Donald Duck mug or bumping against each other to *Dance Party! Volume IV.*

"You mean what their mission is in life?" From where we sit, we can see only the glow of the park and an occasional flash from the shifting castle spotlights.

"I'm serious," I say, dropping my melon rind onto the cement and pulling my knees into my chest with sticky hands.

"Let's hear it."

"I think God ran out of ingredients." I can see Luke out of the corner of my eye, smiling. "He started to make some other type of snail, but when he went to the pantry to get more shells, he realized he was out."

"So why didn't he go to the store?"

"Maybe he was busy. You know, like he thought he'd bust out a couple million snails before lunch, and he didn't have time to drop everything."

"So he decided just to make slugs and call it a day?"

"Maybe he thought no one would notice."

"I don't know, Ella." Luke leans his head back against the bricks and closes his eyes. Another of the reasons I like talking to him is that Luke's smart. And not in that I-can-add-four-digit-numbers-in-my-head smart or I-can-tell-you-the-chemical-equation-of-peanut-butter smart. Luke's smart in the way that I like. In the funny, kind of irreverent, maybe-smarter-than-me smart.

"So, you have a better idea?" I say, making my mouth stay neutral. This is part of our game. Never act too impressed with what the other is saying.

"I think it was more like he had this idea for a new creature, but then when he made the slug, he realized it didn't have any protection."

"So, you think the slug was just the prototype. That the snail is the finished product."

"Exactly," Luke says, turning his head to look at me.

"So why are slugs still around then? Why didn't God just say, 'Whoops, I made a mistake.'"

Luke sighs in an overly dramatic way. "Ella, this is God," Luke says. "He has an image to protect. He can't go around letting everyone know he makes mistakes. 'My bad,' sayeth the Almighty."

"Do you think he does?"

This makes Luke look at me. "What? Make mistakes?"

I'm aware that I'm holding my breath. Luke leans his head back against the wall and stares up into the sky. The castle spotlight swerves back overhead, illuminating his eyes for a moment. The noise behind us gets louder for a second as someone steps out onto the porch.

"Am I interrupting anything?" Cassie asks, and I can tell from her voice she doesn't care if she is or not. Luke turns to look at me for a moment, watching my face.

"Nah," I say, "just taking a break from all the noise." We stay like that for a moment—Cassie glaring at me, and me staring at the lights and willing Luke to get up and go back into the party with her. "So," I say, and it sounds awkward even to me, "where does Jesse get all this stuff?" I point to the beer bottle that is hanging from Cassie's hand. She tilts her head at me as if considering something, then smiles a bit.

"Oh, he has some source in Tomorrowland. Jack something." Luke pushes himself to standing, blocking my view of her for a minute. "He sells it to him at about a twenty-five percent markup. Apparently he has other stuff, too, but I told Jesse no way. With this we might get fired, but I'm not going to risk getting arrested." She presses her lips together, as if willing herself to be quiet.

I don't look at Luke the whole time. I know how this works, and I'm not about to get into a pissing contest with her. As Luke allows himself to be led back inside, I stare straight ahead, watching the beams of light dance. I count slowly between each one, like Ash and I used to do during thunderstorms, marking the seconds between lightning flashes and the first rumblings of thunder. But unlike thunderstorms, where you can estimate their distance, transferring seconds into miles, charting their course, here the lights never vary. Their paths never alter. Their distance never changes.

• • •

"It's weird that you can't seem to remember his name," Amy says, wiggling her fingers up under her wig to scratch her scalp. "I mean, you're with him all the time."

"I can remember," I say, and I can, but not right away. Not until I say some names in my head. "It's Matt." But the look on her face tells me I'm wrong. "Mark."

"I wonder what a psychologist would say about that?" Amy asks.

"Yeah, we work for a place that's run by a giant mouse whose best friend is a duck who doesn't wear pants. I'm thinking forgetting the name of someone I've only known for like three days is not that high on the scale of psychological abnormalities." I've given up being modest, pulling my skirt up to let the fan blow on my legs.

"Nine," Amy says, standing and extending her hand to me.

"Nine what?"

"Nine days. He's been Prince Charming for two more than anyone else." Amy pulls me to standing, and I let my skirts fall back down around my ankles.

"Is it time already?"

"It's already three," Amy says, handing me a water bottle. "You're late for your wedding again."

"Why in God's name are these people here today?" I push aside the curtain that separates the castle staging area from the gardens. Hundreds of people are pressed into the roped-off section. "It has to be a hundred and ten degrees." Outside I can see Mark walking along the roped-off VIP seats. He bends to check the glass slipper he is holding against a girl's foot, making her giggle. He stands and puts his hand to his eyes, scanning the crowd. "Where could she be?" he asks, his voice, magnified by the microphone hidden just beneath his ascot, bouncing off the castle walls.

"That's you," Amy says, fluffing the back of my dress so that it won't stick to my sweaty legs. "See you in a few minutes." Inexplicably, Snow White and Belle are my maids of honor. I have the right to change it up, but only within reason. When Amy wasn't feeling well, I asked if Ariel could stand up for me. Stacy, the princess handler, looked at me like I had just asked if maybe we could sacrifice a live animal during the ceremony. "Ella," Stacy said, her patience obviously at an end, "she's a *mermaid*. She can't be out of the water. She would die."

"Ah, another fair maiden," Matt (no, Mark) says as I step out into the gardens. He pauses as the audience claps, and some guy in the back of the crowd shouts, "Hey, Cinderella, nice rack." To his credit Mark never steps out of character. He *is* Prince Charming. He doesn't have to remind himself to talk vaguely British or not to pull on his pants no matter how much his tights give him a wedgie. "Would'st thou like to try the glass slipper?" I nod slightly and sit on the edge of the rock planter. I don't speak much in these large forums, hating the sound of my voice and the echo it makes. I don't think it matters. No one comes wanting to listen to what Cinderella has to say.

I extend my left foot, letting Mark pull off my shoe. He holds up the glass slipper, which is really made out of a heavy-duty Lucite, for the crowd to see. As he bends to place it on my foot, which I have doused liberally with baby powder so that it will actually go on and not stick on my sweaty toes, the crowd grows quiet. It is in these three or four moments, as everyone is waiting to see if the slipper will fit my foot, that I can see the thing that Walt Disney was trying to get at. The thing that he was trying to box up and portion out for a fee of seventy-five dollars a day. The thing that makes hundreds of thousands of people every year lock up their houses, kennel their pets, freeze their newspaper delivery, and travel hundreds of miles to try and find. It is in the one moment just before my heel slips into the shoe that I, too, pause, watching and waiting, wanting to believe.

"Hey, Cinderella, I got something that'll fit you!"

Mark takes my hand and pulls me to standing. The crowd begins clapping as he drops to one knee to pantomime asking for my hand in marriage. I nod again, this time trying to remember to smile. "This is the happiest day of your life," Stacy reminds me every day as she helps me out of my peasant dress and into my wedding gown.

Out of the corner of my eye, I see the head of a giant chipmunk bobbing over the crowd. As I let Mark lead me toward the castle, where we will prepare for the ceremony, the chipmunk begins waving furiously with both paws. I have to press my hand to my mouth to keep from laughing aloud.

"What are you so happy about?" Amy asks as I step into the tent. She helps me with my zipper and hands me a cool washcloth for my neck.

"Don't you know?" I ask, still smiling. "This is the happiest day of my life."

"Want one?" Mark asks, extending a small box of lemon drops toward me. I take one off the top, rolling it in my fingers before placing it in my mouth. We have to wait offstage while the mice and my fairy godmother finish their musical number. "Think we'll still be here for Cinderellabration?"

"Who knows. I wake up every morning expecting to go home."

"Where is home?" Mark asks, putting the top back on the box of candies. He lifts it to study the gold image of the fairy castle on the side. It's a simple question, but not one with a simple answer.

"Maine," I say softly. "Sort of."

"Sort of?" Mark asks, lifting his eyebrows.

"It's complicated." It comes out more harshly than I intend. Mark blinks a few times before looking back toward where the mice are choosing a girl from the audience to be my flower girl. Stacy told me they used to try to pick a boy to be the ring bearer, but they stopped when some dad freaked out on his wife for trying to *sissify* their son. Mark's fingers begin picking at the castle sticker on the candy box, succeeding in pulling free one corner where it curls away from the plastic, destroying one of the towers. "How about you?" I ask. "Where's home for you?"

"Here," he says, leaning down to place the box in the top of his backpack. He sits up and turns toward me, and the look on my face makes him smile. "I don't mean *here*," he says, opening his hand toward the stones that make up the inside of the castle rooms. "I mean Orlando. About ten minutes from here."

He takes off his crown and runs his fingers through his hair. He turns his head to look at me again, and something in his eyes makes me understand why the other princesses giggle so much when he talks to them. "You know how some families are filled with doctors or lawyers or carpenters?" I nod at him, watching as he turns the crown in his hands. "With my family it's this place."

"Wow," I say softly. "That's rough," but as soon as I say it, I know it's the wrong thing.

"Rough, how?" he asks. "What could be better than this?" and the way he says it is exactly opposite of the way I would say it. The way he says it, I know he means it. Really means it. "Ella, can I ask you something?"

"Sure," I say, but at that moment Stacy walks through the curtains holding my veil.

"You two ready?" she asks. Mark places his crown back on

his head and begins walking toward the stage, where Aladdin and the other prince are waiting for him. Prince Charming's choices for best man are much more limited.

"Ella," Mark says before pushing through the curtains, "in case I forget to tell you later, you look beautiful."

"Well, tell me," Amy asks, bending to unlace her slippers.

"Tell you what?" I ask, pulling the wig from my head and shaking my head to free my hair. I stand in front of the fan, feeling cool for the first time all day. This is the only break that we get. Four hours between the end of the postwedding carriage ride around the park and the Electrical Parade.

"Ella, I haven't known you for very long, but I can tell when something's up."

"It's Mark."

"Oh, it's Mark now, is it?" Amy asks, pulling a T-shirt over her head.

"Very amusing," I say. Amy remains quiet, waiting for me to continue. "He asked me out." I wince a little as I say it, aware of the way Amy is always looking at him.

"That's great," she says, but something in her voice makes me look up. "What about Luke?"

"Luke." I watch her face, but she won't look straight at me. "I don't think he's Mark's type. Besides," I say, "he has a girlfriend." Saying it aloud feels funny.

"He does . . ." Amy says. And I wait for the something more. She tilts her head at me, trying to figure something out, then smiles slightly and shakes her head. "So Mark asked you out."

"Kind of."

"Well, did you say yes?"

I pull off a grape from the basket on the table and pop it into my mouth, buying time. The grapes are a minor victory. Not able to go off campus for fear of being jumped by the picketers, we had to ask management to bring in produce for us. It wasn't until Luke told them that they might not want us all to come down with scurvy that they started bringing in fresh food. There are only so many days that you can live on cheese fries and pizza. "Kind of."

"Okay, Ella. Is it possible for you to be any more vague?"

"Maybe," I say, smiling at her.

"What did you say?"

"I asked him if you could come along." I pull another grape from the bunch and drop it into my mouth.

"Like a chaperone?"

"I thought maybe we could double." She frowns for a moment, looking at the picture on the television at the far end of the room. The images switch every few minutes, showing a live feed of different locations around the park.

"I guess I could ask Jeff," Amy says, still staring at the screen. Teacups swirl across the screen. The camera angle distorts the faces of the people riding in them.

"Jeff? Is he the guy who plays Mowgli? He's cute."

"No, Jeff is Balloo."

"Oh," I say. The screen shifts to a shot of the entrance. I see Chip and Dale facing each other, arms gesturing wildly in what seems to be an argument. "Is he cute?"

"Okay, this is going to sound really strange," Amy says. "I don't know what he looks like. I've never seen him without his costume." She smiles slowly at me. "But he has a great personality," Amy says, hefting her backpack onto her shoulder. I follow her out and toward the nearest monorail platform.

"Get this," I say, stepping under the shade of the canopy to wait for the train, "he's a true believer."

"Who is?"

"Mark. I mean it. He's the real deal. He actually believes in all this junk," I say.

"Ella, there isn't anything wrong with believing in things," Amy says, looking away from me and down the track.

"Sure. Real things. Like saving the rain forest or God or alien abductions, but this is like believing in—"

"What?" Amy asks, looking back at me and tilting her head.

"This is like believing in M&M's, and then finding out when you bite through the shiny colored shell that there isn't anything inside. That there isn't any chocolate. That it's just an illusion."

"That was possibly the worst analogy that I have ever heard," she says, still looking at me intently. "Why does it bug you so much?" she asks finally. "I mean, why do you care what other people believe about this place?" I shake my head and turn down the track to see the monorail slowly making its way around the bend to circle the lagoon. "There's nothing bad in believing, Ella." Amy touches my arm, making me look at her. "Besides," she says, a sparkle in her eyes, "Mark is, as you say, wicked cute."

"So you've told me."

"Have I?" Amy asks, smiling.

"About a hundred times." The tram's brakes squeak as it pulls to a stop in front of us. We wait as a family exits the car, kids licking furiously at ice-cream cones in a losing battle against the heat.

"Well, he is, and he's totally into you," she says, sliding into a seat near the doors. I sit down across from her, letting my pack drop into the seat beside me.

"I don't know," I say, leaning my head against the glass, which is cool against my cheek. "I think maybe it's not so much me he's into. I think it's more Cinderella."

"Well, they do live happily ever after."

"So they say." Across from me, Amy shifts slightly, putting her feet on the seat beside me. I close my eyes, feeling the slow bump of the tram as it slides over the rails. The thing about believing is that it's dangerous. The world can turn upside down in an instant, and just when you think you're on top of everything, you're under it. Believing in something, someone, is hard. Sometimes when you let yourself fall too far, suddenly it's gone.

Luke

The instruction manual says: "After moist toweletting, fluff character hair with the tips of your fingers." I stand back from Dale's body and look at him on his clothes hanger, his head mounted separately beside him. He doesn't really seem that dirty, but one good whiff tells a different story—we sweat *a lot* inside the costumes.

I hold up the manual to Cass. "Finally," I say.

"Finally what?"

"Grammar scientists have solved the problem of turning *towelette* into a verb," I tell her.

"Well, after they perfected *beer me*, it was just a matter of time." She begins blow-drying Chip's topknot of hair, finishing in about ten seconds. The room starts to smell like lemons. I have to devote several extra towelettes to Dale's nose, which gets grubby from all the kisses from children, flirty pats from women, mock punches from men. Most people can't tell us apart by name, but Dale is the one with the red nose and the gap teeth, and is also the stupider of the two, which Cass reminds me of about eight times a day.

This isn't our job, cleaning costumes, but just yesterday the park Garment Care Union went out on sympathy strike. Soon enough the whole park will be on strike. It's getting ugly, and yesterday Jesse was walking through Tomorrowland during his break, just eating a cheese pretzel, and somebody pelted him with a tomato, even though the nearest fence was probably fifty feet away. "You gotta admit," Jesse said, "one of those strikers has a damn good arm." The thing that freaked us all out was that he wasn't even in his Friar Tuck costume, and still they knew he was one of us. "Scabs," they call us when we get near enough to the gate for them to start yelling.

As far as the cleaning goes, face characters have it the easiest, and right now I am half-watching Ella run a steamer over her ball gown, which is hung up with clothespins. Prince Charming (Matt? Mark?) is next to her, combing out the fringe on his epaulets with this old plastic Afro pick he brought with him, the kind with a Black Power fist on the end of the handle. He told us it's the same one his father used to comb out *his* epaulets back in the seventies. I'm betting they are the only father and son in the country sharing this particular tradition. When Cassie razzed him about it, he *quoted* page forty-seven of the manual: "All costume fringe (including epaulets and Davy Crockett's jacket) can be managed using a wide-toothed comb." He had us there. Most of the guys are watching Anna clean her Eeyore costume. She's made herself famous in the space of a week by letting it be known at breakfast that she is usually naked inside her costume. Ella finishes with her three dresses and comes over to help me because I've just discovered a giant wad of gum stuck to Dale's butt. This happens about three times a week, always to Dale, never to Chip. Chip is the serious one, the one who is smart about gathering acorns. No one assaults him with gum.

"Here, Mr. Helpless," Ella says. She reaches into her plastic Donald cup and pulls out an ice cube. Then she sits beside me, and while I stretch the fabric tight across my knee she rubs the ice over and around the wad of gum.

"Would an Afro pick work better?" I say. She smirks.

"Hush," she says, smiling a little. "The ice freezes the gum, then you can just break it off in pieces." She concentrates on what she's doing, her brown hair falling in strands that frame her face. I can feel the pressure of her fingers on my knee, moving in circles, the ice slowly melting in her hand. For half a second all I'm aware of is our breathing.

"Need some help, Luke?" Cass says. She's still holding the blow-dryer, and looks at Ella holding the ice, like there is going to be a battle of the lesser supervillains.

"We're good," Ella says, still concentrating.

Cass looks at me. I shrug and make a face like there's nothing I can do, like I'm trapped here under Ella's fingers, but I feel my face warming, and right now some part of me is wishing that the wad of gum was a foot across, that she was holding a block of ice, and we would be like this for the next two days, just silent, and I could watch her face while she works.

Amy stands near us, retying the sash on her Snow White dress, then untying it and trying again. The manual says it's supposed to "fall naturally," and she keeps complaining that she doesn't know what that means. Finally she gives up, and I hear her muttering curse words under her breath. Ella starts in on the gum with the blade of a butter knife. Cass keeps banging things around in drawers, then cutting her eyes at me when I look up.

"Hey," Amy says, tying her sash again, "what do you guys know about that dude they call the Phantom?"

"Of the Opera?" I say. "I don't think that's Disney."

"No, doofus," she says. "A guy who *works* here. A fur character."

I look around the room while Ella chips away at the gum. No one here looks like a phantom. Matt or Mark is breathing on his brass buttons, then cleaning them with a handkerchief. Robin Hood is making yet another joke about polishing his arrows. It's funny about him—even though his name is Bryan, everyone just calls him by his character name. He just *seems* more like a Robin Hood than a Bryan—not too hard to imagine him stealing from the rich, and keeping it. Big Jesse smacks the dust from his Friar Tuck costume with a broom handle, then practices his English accent by reading the latest memo about how we are all part of the Disney *fahhmily*. Cassie lifts the pole that holds Chip's head. We're supposed to keep them on the poles when we aren't wearing them. She always does, but mine usually ends up on the floor under the bed.

"You should take that outside," I tell her, hoping to make her laugh. "Mount it at the edge of the city as a warning to other striking fur characters."

"That's not funny," Matt/Mark says, still polishing. "Those idiots could shut this place down. They should just be happy they have jobs here."

"Yeah," Ella says, "forget dental insurance. Be happy."

"Wasn't that a song?" Amy says, and everyone laughs. She looks genuinely surprised. Since her arrival she has worked really hard to make friends, and I get the idea that wherever she comes from, she probably isn't all that outgoing. That's the best part of this job. You show up here, then spend half your time being someone you're not. Pretty much like high school, only we get paid for it.

"They will never shut it down," Cass says. "They can't. This place has a life of its own. The people are secondary."

"She's right," Ella says. "It's like McDonald's. Someone quits a place like this, it's like you or me breaking a shoelace." She chips away the last of the gum.

"That's not what I meant," Cassie says.

"So, have you?" Amy says.

"Have we what?" Prince Charming asks her.

She rolls her eyes. "Pay *attention*. Have any of you heard about the phantom guy?"

Just when we start to ask what she's talking about, the loudspeaker crackles on, and Call-me-Bill Tubbs summons us upstairs for another motivational speech. In the background the PA system plays "We Are Family." Mr. Tubbs tells us to have a Disney day.

You can tell all of us are morphing into full-blown adults, wingtip adults, because all the time now the Big Question is, What are you going to do? After the summer, about your scholarship, about choosing a college, after graduation, with the rest of your life. When you are thirteen, the question is, Smooth or crunchy? That's it. Later, at the onset of full-blown adulthood, the Big Question changes a little bit—instead of, What are you going to do? it turns into, What *do* you do? I hear it all the time when my parents have parties, all the men standing around. After they talk sports, they always ask, What do you do? It's just part of the code that they mean "for a living" because no one ever answers it by saying, I go for walks and listen to music full-blast and don't care about my hearing thirty years from now, and I drink milk out of the carton, and I cough when someone lights up a cigarette, and I dig rainy days because they make me sad in a way I like, and I read books until I fall asleep holding them, and I put on sock-shoe, sock-shoe instead of sock-sock, shoe-shoe because I think it's better luck. Never that. People are always *in* something. I'm in advertising. I'm in real estate. I'm in sales and marketing. When Dad gets that question, I always hope he will say, I'm in holes, or I'm in dirt, but he never does. He says that he is in speculative resource development, and most of the time people don't even bother to ask what the hell he means.

It comes up again, that question, during the picnic. After Mr. Tubbs's motivational speech he "surprises" all of us with a picnic lunch, not realizing that the last place we really want to be is outside in the heat again, eating in the town square at the end of Main Street, U.S.A. We sit in the bright grass and on the low stone walls holding our paper plates of wraps and coleslaw and brownies. Cass has been quiet since we were in the laundry room, but she sits so close to me on the brick wall that her thigh is angled up against mine.

"Hi," I say, touching the small of her back.

"Hi." She smirks at me. "I think we'd better make sure this seat is taken." She reaches over and pats my lap with her tanned hand, looking at me.

"What do you mean?" I glance past her long enough to see Ella loading up her plate with food at the tables, laughing at something Prince Charming is telling her.

"We're both smarter than that, Luke," she says. "Do you really want to have the whole conversation?"

I shake my head. "We're just friends, O jealous one," I say. "I think she's funny."

She nods, shrugs. "Okay, how about I find a 'friend' and rub an ice cube up and down his thigh while you watch. Would you like that?" She looks at me over the rim of her cup as she takes a sip of lemonade.

When I picture it, someone else touching Cassie, my stomach knots up. I shake my head again. "No, I guess I wouldn't like that," I tell her. I think back, trying to see myself from the outside, trying to see myself as some shrugging, aw-shucks guy while Ella sits there chipping away at the frozen gum, see myself rolling my eyes at my girlfriend to let her know I don't want to be there any more than she wants me to. I make that picture for myself, but how true is it? I think about what's stored in my head—Ella's hair swaying in shiny strands, Ella's hands with their freckles and veins, Ella's vanilla smell. Even now I want to ask Ella, How true is your memory of an hour? Because I know her answer would interest me. How do you get past the person you think you are if he's always standing in your way? I look at Cass, really look at her, then lean across and give her a kiss, taste the lemon and sugar on her mouth. "I'm sorry," I whisper, but barely hear myself because Ella is laughing behind me.

They sit near us in the grass, Ella and Prince Charming, and Amy right behind them. Mark (he has started wearing his official Disney name tag when we aren't in costume) is telling them more from his storehouse of Disney trivia. Did they know that the only three attractions working on opening day in 1971 were the Swiss Family Treehouse, the Jungle Cruise, and the Tropical Serenade? That only Bill Clinton and George W. Bush recorded their own voices for the Hall of Presidents? He keeps talking, and I keep thinking that he looks like a male model during the Renaissance. Someone says he should be in charge, the new Walt Disney, and he smiles and says he just might, and then there is that question again, What are you going to do?

Jesse says he wants to be a stuntman who specializes in falling from buildings and crashing through walls.

"They specialize?" Amy says, looking at him.

He nods. "Just like doctors except, you know, instead of pediatrics it's like getting shot or walking on trains. The train walking, that's a little hard to practice." On her turn Amy says that she always wanted to teach high school English or band, since she plays the oboe. Prince Charming is going to major in business management. I'm sitting there feeling like we are talking about our Halloween costumes this year, not our entire lives. Why am I not ready for all of this? What's wrong with me? Cassie starts talking then, on and on about Brown, about her scholarship, about her triple major. Her plans seem so much bigger than anyone else's that I can feel the rest of us shrinking in comparison.

Finally it's Amy who interrupts her, though I know all of us, even me, are thinking the same thing.

"What are you doing *here*?" Amy asks her, then blushes.

"I mean, that's not meant to be bitchy or anything. I'm just curious."

Cass smiles. "Listen," she says, "I live in Florida. Around here Disney is like the world's biggest sorority and fraternity, all rolled into one. Later on I just mention this place, it's like I'm part of the club. It'll open doors."

I wonder about that, the idea that the world is just a big private club full of secret doors. I think about how my parents used to be, the ones I see in the photo albums, back when they were attending all the conventions, dressing up in costumes. Back when they were giving me and my brother our oddball names. They weren't much older then than I am now. They are smiling in all those pictures, laughing and silly, until someone told them that they would never be able to join the club if they kept acting like that. "Grow up," someone said, and they did, and they got to join the club, buy the house, own the cars and the pool. The only trade-off—you have to give up the costumes and the laughing.

"Okay, Luke S-stands-for-something Krause," Cass says, "your turn."

"I don't know," I say. "I didn't apply to any colleges, not yet. I don't know what I want to do. Maybe I'll make a career of Dale."

"Like that phantom guy," Amy says.

"He made a career of Dale?"

"No, dumbhead, *you're* Dale. But he made a career of someone. I mean, how much would that suck?"

Cass shakes her head, frowning. "Luke, stop messing around. Tell them about your dad's business."

"You seem to know as much as me. You tell them."

I mean it to be sarcastic, but she doesn't hear it that way, and she starts in telling them about my dad's company, how he went public last year and made all this money in stocks, how he did the drilling for the university, how he started with nothing and made himself rich. "Just like in the movies," she says. I sit there the whole time like I'm Exhibit A, on display. And what can I say? Cass knows all this stuff because I told her all of it the first night I met her. I told her because I was trying to impress her with my father's money and success, like everything he has to show for his life is a flashy car I can borrow and ride around in, honking the horn, pretending it's mine. And the whole time she is talking, I can't look at Ella. For whatever reason, I can't. But I can feel her looking at me.

Cass is finishing her sales pitch of me. "And while we're sitting in a dorm eating ramen noodles," she says, her hand on my shoulder, "this guy is going to be starting out at fifty thousand a year, with his own office, and driving a company truck. I mean, how cool is that?"

All true, all true of Ben before me, all part of my opening night bragfest to Cassie. Now the whole idea of it makes me feel stupid, like all I'll ever do is play grown-up, as opposed to actually growing up. "Well, I don't know," I say before I even realize I'm saying it out loud.

"You don't know what?" Cass says, her hand moving across my back.

"I don't know about any of it. If I want to do that."

"You *have* to do that," she says. "The rest of us would kill for a job like that."

"I hope I'm making that much, like, when I die," Amy says. "I'd buy ten cats and a motorcycle. And a pool."

"Cass is right, dude," Robin Hood says. "Starting at fifty K? That totally rocks."

"I know," I say. "But . . . I don't know. Maybe I just want to do nothing for a while. Just bum around or something. See things."

"Okay, right now we dress up like cartoon characters and shake hands with little kids all day. For minimum wage," Cass says. "*That's* your nothing. That's your bumming around."

"And about a hundred pairs of shoes," Amy says.

Suddenly everyone has joined in, saying I have to take a job like that, just have to, and pretty soon it starts to feel like it does at dinner on Sunday afternoons, when my father and Ben start in talking about the same things: how they will position me, how I need field experience, how much I could learn from six months in the front office. Talking and talking about me, forgetting that I'm sitting there. Cass slides her hand down my arm and squeezes, still talking, while Amy and Jesse keep listing all the things they would buy if they could, and in the middle of all of it, I look over and see Ella, smiling at something Mark is saying to her, but then cutting her gaze at me, holding it, slowly shaking her head while her mouth forms one word: *No.*

Back at the dorm I get messages that I have missed three calls from home. That happens a lot because we are out so much, really just using the dorm for sleep and showers and almost nothing else. Plus, I'm in the costume most of the day and couldn't even take a call if I was sitting right beside the phone. Usually I just avoid the calls because I know what they will be—my mother telling me that this could lead to other acting jobs if I wanted it to, and my father telling me about the latest brilliant thing Ben said in a meeting. I wad up the messages, throw them into the trash.

That night I slip out of the dorm again, the clock tower showing it to be after midnight. And as usual, I find Ella sitting on the bench behind the castle, in the shadows of the leaves. We've met out here twice more since that first night, just sitting and talking—in whispers so we don't get busted. I sit beside her, nudge her knee with mine.

"Luke, I need to tell you—"

"Wait . . . what did you mean today?"

She kicks off a flip-flop, then slides it back on, kicks it off again. "When?"

"At the picnic. Everyone was telling me how great my life was going to be, and you just looked at me and shook your head. You said, 'No.' No what?"

She shrugs. "No, you don't have to listen to them. No, it's

not that great if you don't want it. You know exactly what I meant."

I lean forward, elbows on knees. "Yeah, I guess. But why did you say it?"

She kicks off her shoe again. "I guess I felt sorry for you. Luke, listen—"

My face gets hot. "Felt sorry for me?"

"Everybody ganging up on you. Pelting you with your own success. Yeah, I did." She shrugs again. "Listen, this isn't *Happy Days* and you're not Richie Cunningham having to follow your dad into the hardware business. I'm not the Fonz giving you advice, okay?"

I smile. "You're not?"

"No, I'm way cooler. Look, just do what you want to; it's your life."

"Is that what you're doing? What you want to do?"

She gets very quiet then, and when I look back across my shoulder at her, I see the tears brimming full in her eyes, shining in the dim light. "What I want to do is impossible. Physics and all. Luke, I've been trying to tell you something else—"

I shush her then because I hear footsteps coming. Last time, the security guard found us and spent about twenty minutes explaining the whole concept of curfews. Only this time it's not a security guard, it's Mark walking out of the darkness into all the spilled light in front of the castle.

"What is he—"

"I tried to tell you," Ella says. She shakes her head, wipes her eyes with the back of her hand. "I have to go," she says, then stands and moves off toward him, her flip-flops making their quiet sound against her feet as the clock tower chimes the hour. One chime, then quiet, and they are gone.

Ella

The fact that no one was at the airport to meet me should have been enough to turn me around and send me back to Maine, but the truth was, I didn't have anything to go back to. Our house was empty, a sign from Evergreen Realty poked into the frozen ground. All of our belongings, the ones we didn't sell, were piled in the Rosen's barn. Boxes full of photographs and blankets and china. A tangle of bicycles leaning against one another along the back wall. Snowshoes poking out of milk crates. An apple box stuffed with a camp lantern and empty jam jars. Random items, meant to add up to our lives, waiting in the dusty barn for one of us to come back and find them.

The baggage claim emptied as suitcases were lifted, car seats were unpacked, and golf clubs retrieved. I sat on the top of my suitcase, my blue duffel and backpack leaning against my feet. It had been a long trip. Four planes total—Bangor to Boston. Boston to Atlanta. Atlanta to Orlando. Orlando to Sarasota. It was like spring in fast-forward, snow to sunshine in eleven hours. I stared as the cars slid past, knowing only that Aunt Sara had a minivan. "Blue," my mother said. "Light blue."

For weeks before my trip south, my parents had been reorganizing, regrouping, re-creating. The *re* words had blown into our lives shortly after Ash died. "We just need to reposition, reprioritize, reassess," my father said. Like everything in our lives had been one way, and now it was going to be another. It was as if we'd had a piece of art hanging over our sofa, a painting of the ocean with a setting sun, the sky bright with reds and oranges and yellows, then one day someone came in and told us it was upside down. That instead of the ocean, the blue was actually the sky, and instead of a sunset, the bright colors were actually a meadow filled with flowers.

It was my mother who first broke the news. "Cameroon," she told me, and for a second I thought she was talking about coconut cookies. "It's in Africa. West Africa, near Nigeria." And suddenly, the vague ideas about their doing something for others and making a difference in the world had details and a date. The talk about Third World countries and famine and the AIDS epidemic had focus and an itinerary.

"When are you going?" I asked, thinking late summer or fall. Sometime after I left for college.

"In six weeks," she said. "March nineteenth." She paused slightly, as if the reality of what they were doing had forced its way past passport photos, vaccinations, language lessons, and mosquito netting. "It took us by surprise, too, Ella," she said, fiddling with the blanket folded on the foot of my bed. And the way her voice sounded, I knew by "it" she meant Ash.

"What about me?" I asked, but I knew the answer was the one I had already realized. Instead of pulling together, circling the wagons against our pain, my parents had drifted away. Like parental attachment in reverse. "What about school?" I was still three months short of high school graduation.

"They said they'd let you graduate early."

I tilted my head at her. There was something else there. Something she hadn't told me yet.

"Aunt Sara said you could live with her until you start at Vermont."

"In Florida?" I asked.

"We thought you'd love it." I sat and watched my mother touching the satin edge of my blanket, smoothing it between her thumb and her forefinger, sliding her fingers past one another along the fold. "No school. No responsibilities. Just time to relax."

"Just think of it as an extended vacation before you have

to buckle down again in the fall," my father said from the doorway. They waited in silence, my mother still rubbing the edge of my blanket, my father leaning against the jamb. I wondered briefly what would happen if I just said no. Would they stay? Would they realize that instead of losing one child, they were in ways losing two?

"Okay," I whispered, knowing that no matter where I was, Florida or Maine or Cameroon, nothing was going to fix what was really wrong. Nothing was going to change the fact that my brother was gone, and that even when they were right there in my room, sitting on my bed and standing there in my doorway, my parents were gone, too.

I remember hearing the van before I saw it, wheels squealing on the hot asphalt as it took the corner too fast. It came to an abrupt stop in front of where I was sitting under the overhang of the terminal, out of the sun, but not out of the heat. The automatic door slid open. Out spilled the theme song from *Blue's Clues* and an empty juice box. "Get in," said Aunt Sara, leaning back in the driver's seat to peer out the door. "Quick, before they wake up." I didn't know who "they" were until I leaned into the back of the van to position my suitcase behind the passenger's seat. "They" were three children. A boy, a girl, and an infant of unknown gender. All in car seats, all asleep. I pulled my hand back and watched the door close in front of me. As I slid into the passenger seat and pulled my seat belt across my lap I had the sinking feeling that maybe my time at Aunt Sara's was not going to be quite as advertised. Words like *relax, regroup, reprioritize* seemed like they were about to morph into *rediaper, re-dress, redirect,* and *regurgitate.* Suddenly six months in Florida seemed like a really long time.

"Bend down and look at the statue," Mark says. I bend slightly, peering at the figure of Cinderella. "Lower. Think six-year-old child." I bend farther, nearly kneeling in front of the bronze statue, this one featuring Cinderella in her peasant dress. The soft splashing of the fountain to her left invites anyone with a penny to make a wish. "Do you see it?" he asks. I squint at the statue, looking into the folds of her dress and the curls of her hair for an answer.

"Mark, I'm sorry. I don't—"

"Ella," he says, kneeling just behind me. "Not at her. At the castle." He places his hands on either side of my head, letting his fingers rest against the curve of my jawline, and tilts my head upward slightly. I look past her kerchiefed head to the mural painted on the castle wall. Then I see it. A crown, hovering there, just over the statue's head.

"I see it," I say, feeling his fingers on my neck, hot against my skin.

"See?" he says, letting his fingers trail through the back of my hair. He takes my arm and pulls me to standing. "She was a princess even before anyone knew it." I turn to face him, feeling the mist from the fountain blowing over us in the breeze. He leans toward me, and I close my eyes. I feel the brush of his lips on mine, so soft that for a moment I'm not even sure if he's actually kissed me or if I've just imagined it. The flags snap in the air overhead as the wind picks them up. Then the press again, a little harder, more solid, more sure. He places his fingertips on my jawline again, this time letting them trace the side of my neck and brush my collarbone.

I concentrate on kissing him back, moving my lips against his. And I realize that I *do* have to think about it, concentrate on it, because I find my mind wandering . . . back to the look on Luke's face when he saw Mark walking toward us in the dark. And from there I start to think about Luke in general, that I told him to follow his heart. What a crock that is. Like I'm some sort of expert.

"That was nice," Mark says, leaning his forehead against mine. He's right. It was nice, not nice in the way that I want a kiss to be, but nice in the "having lunch with you was nice" or "she seems nice" or "a glass of lemonade on a hot day is nice" way. And I realize I should say something, too.

"It was," I say.

"Ella," Mark says, leaning back so that he can look at me, "I like you." I tilt my head at him and wonder how that can be. How can you like something you don't know anything about? But the way he says it with that earnest look on his face, which he seems to have about just about everything, makes me nod at him.

"Me too," I say, and it's true. I do like him. I like him,

and kissing him is nice. And maybe for now that's enough, because maybe letting someone know me past the costume, past this summer, past this very moment, is just too much. He leans toward me again, but I turn slightly so that I'm looking back at the castle. His lips brush at my cheek.

"You know, yesterday when I was walking down the aisle, I thought I saw someone." Mark follows my gaze, looking up at one of the narrow windows in the towers. "Do you think it's haunted?" I've been thinking about this all day, how sometimes things aren't what they seem.

"Maybe by Roy Disney," he says, and it makes me look at him, surprised to hear him make a joke. I smile at him, but he continues. "There's an apartment built inside the castle. I hear the bigwigs use it for parties." I turn back to look at the castle, framed by the dark sky. I guess I have to amend my thoughts. Apparently, sometimes things are just what they seem.

"Well, it's instead of playing quarters again," Amy says.

"Tell us the rules," I say, not so much because I want to play, but because I am tired of quarters and tired of everyone just getting drunk and stupid and making out in corners. I think the only one in the room besides me that's on Amy's side is Jesse, and that's only because he's shy half a head of hair and one eyebrow after the other Merry Men found him passed out in the bathroom.

"It's easy. You just write down one secret on a card. One that no one knows about. Then we put all of the cards into this hat," Amy says, lifting her set of mouse ears with SNOW WHITE stitched in curly yellow thread across the back. A gift from Jeff on our double date.

"So when do we drink?" Anna asks. Most of the guys laugh, probably less because it's funny and more because they're hoping to make some time with Winnie-the-Pooh's melancholy friend.

"I'd like to help her find her tail," whispers Buzz Lightyear.

Amy keeps on talking, probably thinking the same thing I am. That anyone dumb enough to get into her costume naked can't really spare any brain cells. "One at a time I'll draw a card and read the secret. Then everyone has to guess whose secret it is."

"Sounds fun," Luke says, and I look over at him, but he won't meet my gaze. Ever since that night in front of the castle, he's been going out of his way to avoid me. Or maybe he's just not going out of his way to see me. It's not like Dale has that many reasons to interact with Cinderella.

Amy passes out the index cards and pencils with Mickey and Donald eraser toppers. I get Mickey. The room gets quiet as everyone thinks of a secret to write on their card. Only Mark seems to know one right off, scribbling on his card, which is propped on the arm of the couch beside him.

"No fair telling us something lame. Like you have a secret desire for green olives," Cassie says from where she is sitting on the floor in front of Luke.

"Unless you like to have green olives during sex," one of the Merry Men says from the other side of the pool table.

"Gross," Anna says, making Amy cut her eyes at me. From what we've seen, nothing seems to be off-limits for her.

"Hush," Devin says. She has her long hair pulled up in a bun on the back of her head. It's so dark and shiny, they just let her use her real hair instead of wearing the Jasmine wig they gave her. She's so beautiful that part of me wanted to dislike her right off the bat, but she's nice, too, giving everyone cookies from the care packages her mother sends her and always smiling; you can't help but like her. Mark gets up and walks over to where Amy has the hat sitting on the table. He drops his folded card into it and picks the hat up by one of the ears, passing it to Jesse, who's leaning against the wall. I tap my pencil against the card as I watch the hat make its way through the cluster of Army Men from *Toy Story* sitting around the pool table and then out onto the porch, where my fairy godmother is too busy kissing Goofy to notice.

"Ahem," Cassie says, separating the couple long enough for them to drop their cards into the hat. Most of my secrets are too stupid. Like, I still sleep with the blanket I got when I was six. I write half an answer, then stop and tap my pencil's Mickey head against my lips. I bite down hard on Mickey's ear and look over at where Luke is sitting. He's not writing, either. He's staring past me through the sliding glass doors, his card dangling from his fingers. Cassie waves her hand in front of his eyes, breaking his concentration. His lips twitch

slightly, and he considers his card again, but as soon as Cassie turns away, he looks up. This time directly at me. I think he's going to look away again, like he's been doing for more than a week now, but he doesn't. And we sit there looking at each other until I feel a bump against my arm. The hat. I panic and drop my card in before I have anything much written down. I look up again, but Luke is back to staring at the card on his knee. I watch as the hat makes its way toward him. Cassie takes the hat, drops her card in, then snatches Luke's card and drops his in, too. He starts to say something, but then he just shrugs and frowns. The hat makes its way all the way back to Amy, who drops her card in.

"Who wants to do the honors?" she asks, dipping her hand in and mixing the cards.

"You do it," Jesse says from the floor. He's now lying flat on his back, his eyes closed. Amy places the hat on the table in front of her and takes out a card.

"Okay," she says, "first secret." She looks at me and raises her eyebrows, but before she can read it aloud, someone bangs on the door.

"EMERGENCY MEETING," a voice booms from the hall—one of the chaperones not wanting to come in and witness anything they actually have to address. "EVERY-ONE TO THE CONFERENCE CENTER. TEN MIN-UTES." The room gets quiet for a moment, but soon everyone is talking at once. Pulling on sandals and throwing away beer bottles.

"I wonder if they settled the strike?" Mark asks, coming up behind me and placing his hand on the small of my back.

"I wonder if they found out about the fountain," Jesse says, making the Merry Men laugh. I watch as Amy takes the inverted mouse ears full of our deepest secrets upstairs to our room.

Luke slides past me, and I almost say something, but I see Cassie on his other side, pulling him away from me. We all walk together in twos and threes across the courtyard and past the teacups, no longer spinning, grouped together as if waiting for giants to come and sip from them.

"What do you think?" Amy asks, catching up to me and looping her arm through mine.

"I don't know," I say, and I realize that of all the things I've been thinking and saying and doing, that's about as honest as I can be. I just don't know.

Luke

Suddenly, Amy is cornering the market in secrets. First she claims to have more info about the Phantom, although the details, she says, are "less than sexy." A little hung over among the eggs and frozen waffles and dreading a day ahead in the Florida sun, everyone just looks at her and nods.

"But still," she says, stirring a third teaspoon of sugar into her coffee, "I did find out some stuff. The guy is a fur character, J. Worthington Foulfellow, and he's played him since the first year the park opened in, like, 1972. I mean, that's almost as long as my dad has been *alive*. He lives in a trailer parked behind the shed where they store cat litter for cleaning up oil spills and vomit."

"Your dad?" someone says.

Amy gives this little grunt of disgust. "No, the *phantom* guy. Pay attention."

"That's all?" I say. "How does that make him the Phantom in any sense of the word?"

Amy doesn't back down. "He lurkssss around the park at niiiight." She makes her eyes big and draws out each word like she's narrating *The Twilight Zone*.

"Soooo dooo I . . ." I say to her.

"Wow," Jesse says to her in a deadpan, "you're just like Nancy Drew."

"Shut *up*," she says, and smacks his arm.

Jesse raises both eyebrows, except that he doesn't have any eyebrows, so he just wrinkles up his forehead. He shaved the other one off himself after the first was taken from him in his sleep. When I asked, he said, "There is beauty in symmetry," and kept shaving.

"Okay, excuse me?" Anna says. "But who is J. Worthington Foul Whatever? Is that, like, Peter Pan?"

"Good question," Robin Hood says, nodding. "And furthermore, do you think he's naked inside his costume?" Anna seems not to realize this is directed at her.

"J. Worthington Foulfellow is from Pinocchio," Mark says, gesturing with his fork. "Also known as Felonious Fox. He wears a tattered vest and a top hat, carries a brass cane." Ella leans into him and smiles, like she is really impressed by his encyclopedic knowledge of Disney crap. I think maybe that's his calling, that one day Matt/Mark will publish *The Big Book of Disney Crap,* and I almost say it, but don't. I just know that she is smarter than that, and that right now she ought to be looking at me across the table and rolling her eyes at Prince Dork, not smiling at him admiringly like he just cured cancer—in his head, over a plate of eggs. So why isn't she?

"I just think it's strange," Amy says. "You never see him."

"Maybe he's Walt Disney's secret love child," Jesse says, still chewing. "Hidden away forever inside his costume. Oh, dear *God*!" He says this last part loud enough that everyone stops for a second and looks at him, all of us laughing.

Except Ella.

I watch her, and while everyone laughs, she just half smiles. And it's not like she is all depressed, unable to laugh, but more like she is only half here. Half-listening. Half-laughing. I think how pretty she is, her brown hair falling in strands around her face, her arms freckled from the sun, her green eyes flecked with bits of copper, and I wonder where her other half is, *what* her other half is, that keeps her from really being here. I can see it in the way she sits there, pulled into herself. Or like the way someone's eyes lock onto nothing when they're caught in a daze, except that's not how she is, exactly. Her gaze is locked onto *something,* and it makes her eyes soft and distant, like she is looking at her own phantom, something far off and invisible that none of the rest of us can see, that she can't stop looking at. I want to know what it is, and right then, sitting there over bacon scraps and cold coffee, I have to resist the urge to lean across and just ask her. But that's not my job, I guess. I'm not the one walking off with her into the shadows of the castle. I think about that, about how that night felt when Mark walked out of the shadows and she left me, and suddenly I'm fighting back tears, blinking my eyes, pretending like I have something in them.

Amy isn't done talking about secrets. She still has the mouse hat filled with everyone's card.

"I feel like God," she says. "I know everything."

"Hey, God," Robin Hood says, "lower the temperature by thirty degrees, okay? And make all the moms today be babes."

Amy smiles. "I will take that under advisement."

"It's not like the cards are a big deal," Jesse says. "I mean, you don't know who wrote them. You have limited omniscience."

"Because that's so hard to figure out," Amy says, smiling.

Jesse rolls a pancake around his scrambled eggs, then eats it like a wrap. "Well," he says, chewing, "that's my point. It is hard."

"My sweet Jesse," Amy says. "You know, Jesus will be royally pissed that you stole forty dollars from the collection plate when you were twelve."

"Well, he's your son," Robin Hood says. "Tell him to settle down."

Jesse chews and nods, blushing. "Okay, lucky guess. Or likely guess, I should say."

"You will *never* guess mine," Anna says. She adjusts the green bikini top she always wears to breakfast and smiles at us. Amy just cuts her eyes at the rest of us and slowly shakes her head.

Finally Ella does catch my eye across the table and gives me a smile with just the corner of her mouth. I know that she thinks I'm all mad at her after that night, that I'm jealous. And it probably seems that way because since that night I have been all over Cassie, giving her constant attention, telling her we should go to the beach for a week when they finally let us out of here. I even bought her a little garnet ring in the gift shop for our one-month anniversary. So, to Ella, I'm like some guy in a stupid teen movie, the guy who plays it up big with some new girl because he's jealous, because he just wants to put the other person's face right in it—*see what you missed?* All a game, and at the end, you know the boy and girl will get together. But this isn't like that. "Life is not a movie," my father used to say all the time, and he should know. The only girl I will get is the one I have. That's how it's supposed to be, right? Date the right girl, take the right job. It's like a Zen riddle—why do you do what you're supposed to do? Because it's what you're supposed to do. And Cassie? She's perfect. Chip and Dale makes sense. Cinderella and Dale? No one wrote that story yet. No one ever will.

"So, Luke," Ella says, "what was on your card?" I know

she's saying this for the whole table, but somehow, when I glance up, she is really *looking* at me, like she wants to see into me, into my bones and heart.

"His middle name," Jesse says. "The biggest secret of them all."

"Not bloody likely," I say, smiling. I glance back at Ella, and she is still looking at me, waiting for my answer. Just then Cassie shows up carrying her tray—nothing but fruit—and she sits beside me.

"Morning, you," she says, and lifts her hand to give my hair a little tug in back, then leans over for a kiss.

"You guys should switch to Tweedledee and Tweedledum," Ella says. "Then you'd have built-in pet names. 'Dale' is a little low on the cuteness factor."

I look at Ella, trying to catch her eye, wanting just then to take her away and tell her what I started to write on my card before I ran out of time, or maybe to ask what she wrote on hers. And I know this isn't her, either—playing at the jealousy thing like there is going to be some sniping catfight. When she gets like this, pulled back, taking potshots at people, I know, *know*, that something is really bothering her.

"I was wondering," Cassie says, "when you sing 'Someday My Prince Will Come,' is that like a single entendre?" Jesse laughs, but most of the others seem not to get it.

Ella just frowns at her bowl of Cheerios and looks at me as she gets up from her seat. "Nice girl," she says.

We all watch her leave. Finally Mark thinks to get up and

follow her, and I convince myself not to. "What a freak," Cassie says, sliding her hand along my thigh. Mark runs out after her, the same stagy, practiced run he uses during the wedding every day, and I think for half a second that when he gets outside, all he will find is her shoe, lost on the cafeteria stairs. That seems about right, the same story getting told over and over, and everyone knows how it ends.

I finally talk to Ben that afternoon on the phone. He tells me that he and Dad were supposed to go to Brazil next week to look over a job site, but they had to cancel because Dad isn't feeling too well.

"And Mom?" I say.

"She hasn't dug out the biohazard suit yet," he tells me, and I laugh. The whole time we were growing up, she was the most squeamish person you could imagine. One time, when I was seven, I threw up in the living room, and she just put an upside-down bucket over it and called a cleaning service. And when any of us were sick, she went around the house in yellow rubber gloves, like the kind you use to wash dishes. A scraped knee meant she just handed over the box of Band-Aids. Later on, if we wanted to be left alone, all we had to do was *act* like we were about to throw up. Now it's Dad, who is *never* sick, and I can only imagine how freaked-out she is.

"Did Dad hurl? Did Mom move to a hotel yet?"

He laughs. "Nah. He keeps saying it's headaches. The doctor thinks it's just tension or heatstroke from golf. I think it's too much work. He works all the time. See, if this was next year, I'd manage the job site, and you'd be coming with me."

I nod at the phone until I remember that Ben can't see me. "Yeah, I guess that's right."

"It'll be next year soon enough," he says, and I feel my stomach knot up. I lean against the wall by the pay phone and glance down the hall, where Robin Hood is carrying in yet another case of beer. I'm getting a little tired of all the parties.

"Ben, are you still playing the guitar?"

"When I can. I suck, though."

"Yeah, you do. Still driving the Honda?"

"Luke, you've been gone, what? Six weeks? You sound like some grandpa who wants to visit the Old Country before he dies or something. Are you homesick?"

"Nah," I say, but in a way I am. I guess I'm thinking about the photo albums from when Mom and Dad used to go to the conventions and stuff, and how they were in the newspaper for the names they gave us, and how they still keep their costumes in the attic. And then I think how long it's been since we even looked at the photo albums themselves, so that the thing I feel homesick for is the time when we *wanted* to look at the pictures, when we still cared about what was in them. Maybe there should be photo albums with pictures of when you used to look at your photo albums. I think about saying this to Ben, but I know he wouldn't get it.

And neither would Cassie, and maybe no one would. Then I think no, I could tell Ella, and she would get it. I wish I *could* tell her.

"Well, get your ass home," Ben says, "and I'll show you where your office is going to be next year. You have a better window than I do."

"That's great," I say. And I try, really hard, to believe it.

That night all the girls decide they are going to move down to the second floor of the dorm and have "girls' night," which means . . . I don't really know. None of us do, though we guess. Like maybe they are going to paint toenails and braid hair and talk about guys and eat chocolate.

"Yeah, right," Robin Hood says, "and they're going to read *Tiger Beat,* too. You guys are lame."

"What do you think they're doing?" Jesse says. He goes to the fridge and starts handing out cans of beer. The other Merry Men and the Army Men start arguing about their characters, who could beat whose ass.

Robin Hood shrugs. "I'm thinking white wine and naked pillow fights."

"Okay, that was supposed to be a guess," I tell him. "We're not probing your fantasy life." I take a slice of cold pizza from the box that's going around.

"I'm a man," he says, leaning back against the couch while he eats. "I think manly thoughts."

"Yeah, you're a man," I say, laughing. "Yellow tights and kelly green tunic, dead giveaways."

He throws a pillow at me. "And you're what? Some androgynous rat?"

Jesse fires the remote at the TV, and for a few minutes we quiet down and watch a baseball game. Robin Hood keeps saying that all the players are lame, while Mark surfs some website about the history of the park and throws out little tidbits to us about our characters or where the least crowded bathrooms are. The Army Men and the Merry Men are across the room playing darts, or playing some drinking game that involves darts. The pizza box comes around again, and Robin Hood clicks around the channels until he settles on the Home Shopping Network, then he borrows Jesse's cell phone to call the hotline and talk to the hosts. He gets through right away and tells them that he lost over 480 pounds using the Total Gym, while the rest of us try to keep from laughing behind him. Right there on the screen, the hosts are shaking their heads, telling him how amazing that is. Half an hour later he calls back and tells the new hosts that he now makes *all* of his family's meals using the Solar Grill. He goes on and on about it, then, right before he hangs up, says that the Solar Grill is the greatest invention since the polio vaccination.

Jesse gets up and hands everyone another beer. "Man," he says, "we should just go *down* there. Crash the party."

"Okay, normally I would be all in for that," Robin Hood says, "but they would be way, way pissed. You heard them."

Mark looks up, takes a sip of his beer, and asks us if we realize that there are over twenty thousand different colors of paint used inside the park. The rest of us mutter something along the lines of *Wow, that's amazing.* As much as I want to hate the guy, there is something so earnest about him that I can't; none of us can. He always acts like some little kid who found a lizard and brought it to school for show-and-tell.

Robin Hood looks over at me. "Dude, you must be hurtin' tonight."

"Why?"

He shakes his head. "Cassie? Hello? Man, you're, like, my hero, hooking up with that chick."

I feel my face heating up. "Yeah," I say, "she's pretty cool."

Robin Hood looks at Jesse, then jerks his head toward me. "Get him . . . 'pretty cool.' Dude, the girl is gorgeous as hell, she's smart . . ." He shrugs. "It's a long list."

"Yeah, Luke," Jesse says. "How come you and not me? It's that mysterious middle name thing, right? Like you seem all dangerous and secret. I gotta remember that."

"Yeah, try it," I tell him, looking down at my beer, wanting nothing more than for this conversation to end. I feel . . . I don't know. Fake, somehow. But Robin Hood isn't done yet.

"You know, here's the thing." He lifts the remote and mutes the TV. "Like Anna, that chick is hot and all, but she's kinda slutty and just way too girly, you know? But Cass, man . . . she could be here right now, just hanging with the boys, kicking it, you know?"

"Yeah, I know," I say. And I do know. Everything he says about her. She seems perfect. But it's that word *seems*, like I have to see her from the outside, I have to *realize* she's perfect.

"Now, I'll tell you who I don't get," Robin Hood says, and leans in so just me and Jesse can hear him talk. "Ella. Ella comma Cinder. I do not understand the wavelength involved there."

When he says her name, I feel like I can't breathe, and I want to think that she is downstairs right now, on a similar couch, not breathing because someone has said my name, but I know that's not how it is. She's downstairs wondering if it's time yet to meet Mark under the clock tower.

"I don't know," I say. "She's cool. I mean, she's pretty funny."

"Yeah, like she gets off a good line, then five minutes later looks like she's headed to a funeral. We were fine the first day, then later I tried to talk to her and it was like I had leprosy or something. I mean, I was just *talking*, dude, you know?"

I nod.

"She likes *you*, though," Jesse whispers. "I don't know your secret, man. If you got rid of Prince Doofus, you could have your pick. Maybe you should stage a coup."

"Yeah, like that choice would take all of a nanosecond,"

Robin Hood says. "Really, man, major props." He raises his beer can. "Here's to you, dude." Jesse raises his as well, and I have no choice but to do the same. We drink to me, to how lucky and happy I am. By now the beer is warm, and I swallow hard to get it down.

Ella

God, another meeting. That makes four this week. I have the urge to remind management about "The Boy Who Cried 'Wolf.'" What if there is a *real* emergency, like a total power outage or maybe a hurricane? It's all because Mr. "Call me Bill" Tubbs got promoted to Vice President for Vendor Relations, which sounds flashy but apparently is pretty much about making sure they have enough hot dogs before a big weekend and that the cost of glow-in-the-dark necklaces stays below five dollars.

"I wonder what Estrogen wants this time?" Robin Hood asks, sitting down on the other side of Amy. I raise my eyebrows at him. "That's what the Army Men started calling her after the last meeting," he says. Evelyn "Don't call me anything but Ms. Burrows" Burrows came down on them pretty hard about their marching songs, telling them to at least keep them PG rated. *Whether right or whether wrong/ Army men are really hung.*

"I am so tired," Anna says, stretching her arms over her head in front of us.

"Man," Amy says, leaning into me. "Could she be any more slutty?"

"I hope so," Robin Hood says. Amy gives him an elbow, making him laugh. "What, are you jealous?"

"*Ew,*" Amy says.

"There's plenty of me to go around."

"I said *ew.*"

"I'll second that," Cassie says, sitting down in front of her. Luke follows her, smiling slightly at me before he sits down.

"Ladies, please," Robin Hood says, leaning back and stretching his legs out in front of him, so they are nearly all the way under Cassie's chair. "No fighting." Amy rolls her eyes in my direction.

Evelyn walks in carrying a large cardboard box and sets it on the table at the front of the room. "Okay, people," she says, looking up at us. "Let's settle down." She pulls several packets out of the box and lines them up on the edge of the table. "We have recently had some complaints."

"Uh-oh," Jesse says, leaning forward in an attempt to hide behind Luke.

"What did you do?" Robin Hood whispers, but Jesse just shakes his head.

"In the past three days we have received seventeen guest comment cards regarding lack of park knowledge on the part of the cast."

Jesse sits up again and smiles. "*Whew*," he whispers, looking over at us.

"What did you *do*?" Amy asks.

"Tell you later," Jesse says, winking at her. I waggle my eyebrows at her when she looks at me, making her blush. Evelyn clears her throat from the front of the room, looking over at our section.

She shuffles some cards in her hand. "Just a sampling," she says. "On Friday a family of four missed Cinderella's wedding after they were told it was at four instead of three. On Saturday evening two children were told that Ariel is a fish." Evelyn shuffles the cards again, apparently searching for one in particular. "Sunday morning a tour group from Japan was told that Mickey was not at breakfast, because he'd had a hard night and needed to—quote—sleep it off." She delivered this last one without taking her eyes off Robin Hood. "People, this is not the image that we want to present here. Normally, I would tell you to read your employee manuals more carefully or attend one of our cast orientation seminars, but as we all know . . . these are not normal circumstances." I see Mark nodding like mad beside me. "So after consulting with my staff, I believe we have reached a solution." She lifts one of the packets from a stack in front of her. "We have decided that there are two main problems."

"The heat and the heat," Jesse whispers. I see Amy nodding in his direction. He looks over at her again and smiles.

"It seems that we have a general lack of staff cohesion."

"That sounds like an STD," Robin Hood whispers before Amy shushes him. Evelyn looks over in our direction, and Robin Hood sits forward slightly, as if hanging on her every word. She raises an eyebrow at him before continuing.

"I have devised a solution that will tackle both the lack of morale and the apparent lack of Disney knowledge." Evelyn takes off her glasses and lays them on the table in front of her.

"All the better to see you with," Robin Hood whispers.

"Starting today and continuing over the next three weeks until Cinderellabration, we will be having a cast member scavenger hunt. The grand prize is two days off with pay." Everyone begins murmuring at once. "And two nights in the guest accommodations of your choice anywhere in the park. Epcot included."

"Sweet," Robin Hood says, lifting his hand in Jesse's direction for a high five.

"However, there are some rules." Everyone quiets down as she puts her glasses back on. "First rule, you will be competing in pairs." Cassie stands and actually knocks over her chair.

"Holy shit, Cass," Robin Hood says, pushing her chair back upright and out of his lap.

Cassie leans down and says something in Luke's ear. He

grabs her arm, but she shakes it off and turns to push past me to where Mark is sitting.

"Competitive much?" Robin Hood asks.

"What do you say, Mark?" Cassie asks. He looks at me, but I just shrug. "Okay?" Cassie is almost breathless, making me cut my eyes at Amy.

"Nice girlfriend you got there, Luke," Robin Hood says, slapping him on the back. Luke ignores him, but I can tell he's mad.

"Up to you," I say to Mark. He looks at me for a moment before nodding. I turn toward Amy. "Want to be my partner?" I ask.

"I think you're already spoken for," she says, smiling at me.

"By who?" I ask, but Luke is looking right at me. He tilts his head slightly in my direction.

"You sure?" I say to Amy.

"Totally," she says, squeezing my hand. I nod at Luke, and he goes to the front of the room to retrieve our packet.

"So, who're you going to be with?" I ask. "Jeff?" I look over to where he is sitting with Mowgli, but he isn't looking our way.

"Yeah, remember how I kept telling you that he was always such a gentleman when we did things together?" I nod, still watching as Jeff gets up to walk to the front of the room, too. "Well," she says, lowering her voice, "let's just say that Jeff is a lot more interested in princes than princesses."

I raise my eyebrows at her. "Sorry," I say.

"No big. It's not like I had ordered the invitations or any-thing." She smiles at me.

"So, darlin'," Jesse says, leaning across Robin Hood's lap, "you and me?" Amy nods and I see her blush again.

Evelyn claps from the front of the room, lowering the volume slightly. "We are providing each team with a digital camera, courtesy of the marketing staff. You will be respon-sible for the care of this equipment, and any damages or loss will be taken out of your paycheck."

"Anna," Robin Hood says, pushing Jesse away and lean-ing forward, "what do you say you and I pair up?" She just giggles and nods at him.

"Since winning's out of the question," he says, leaning back and stretching his arms across the backs of the chairs, "might as well have some fun."

"Yo, Robin," one of the Army Men yells. "The camera's for the scavenger hunt, not to fill your website with naked pictures."

"I resent thine comment," he says, still lounging back in his chair, leaving Anna to go retrieve their packet and their camera.

"More like you resemble it," Jesse says, making the whole room laugh. Luke comes back from the front of the room and takes the chair that Mark has vacated. He and Cassie have relocated to the front of the room, right in front of Evelyn.

"Once you have your packet, please take a seat so that I can go over the rest of the rules," Evelyn says. We all wait several more minutes while the last remaining people pair up and get their stuff. "Okay, then," Evelyn says, picking up one of the packets left in the messy heap on the table. "First, the grand prize will be given to each member of the team. That means that each person will receive the two-night stay for her and the guest of her choice. Or his choice," she finishes, looking directly at Mark. "Furthermore, if you are thinking that you can just halve the list, letting each of you work independently, listen up." I watch Cassie stop pulling apart her packet. "In order to get credit for an item, you must not only take a picture of the item but *both* of you must also be in the photo." A couple of people groan from the back of the room. "This is to ensure that *all* of you do the work." She looks significantly at Robin Hood when she says this. Mark raises his hand.

"Yes?" Evelyn says, looking at him over the top of her glasses.

"What if we find everything on the list before the time is up?"

"Well, seeing as how the list has over seven hundred items on it, I don't think that is very likely." She smiles slightly at him, the most emotion she has shown since she took this position. "Now, some of the items are intentionally vague, giving you the chance to be creative. For instance, say the list says 'Lion's Head'—this isn't actually on your list," she says, making Cassie stop shuffling her pages. "There are many possibilities. You might choose to take a photo of one of the plush Simba toys in the gift shop, or a picture of the dancer in the *Lion King* show, or maybe even the animatronic lion in the Jungle Cruise ride. Does that make sense? The idea is to make you more familiar with your surroundings, and that will benefit our guests." She looks around the room. I glance over at Luke, who's fiddling with our camera. He manages to take a picture of his foot.

"I think we're in trouble," I whisper, elbowing him.

"Hush," he says, smiling at me.

"The deadline is midnight after the final Cinderellabration Electrical Parade. All searching should be done during your off-hours, and never in costume. You will turn in your cameras directly to me. My staff and I will go through them, checking off your lists. When we have a winner, we will call a meeting to announce it."

"What does second place get?" Robin Hood asks.

Evelyn takes off her glasses and looks directly at him. "There is no prize for second place."

"Whoa," Jesse whispers. "She's intense." Robin Hood is actually quiet for a moment, then he smiles.

"I know," he says, leaning back in his chair again. "That's hot."

"All right, if there aren't any other questions . . ." She looks around the room again. "Good luck."

"Yeah, like they're going to need it," Robin Hood says, looking over at Cassie and Mark already heading out the door. "Mr. Disney." He stands and stretches his arms over his head before sliding past us. "Sorry, dude," he says, clapping Luke on the shoulder as he passes. We watch him slide his arm around Anna's waist and lead her out the door.

"I'm not," Luke says, without looking at me. *Me neither,* I say, but only to myself.

"You sure you're not mad?" Mark asks. I shake my head. "What, then?" he asks, pointing over to a bench. We've been wandering along the Main Street for the last hour or so, trying to stay out of the sun by ducking into the shops.

"I don't know," I say, but the truth is, I do, and it has nothing to do with Mark or Cassie or the scavenger hunt.

"It just happened so fast," Mark says. I take a sip of my lemonade and watch as Rabbit attempts to pull the honey-pot off Winnie the Pooh's head. "I just think Cassie wants to win," he says. "I mean, if it weren't for the fact that she had to work, we'd already be at it."

"I guess," I say. Rabbit succeeds in pulling the pot from Pooh's head, making the crowd cheer. "I just don't understand why you didn't think *we* could win."

"I think it was more that she didn't think Luke could win. I mean, he's not the most motivated person in the world." I can tell from his voice that Mark is just making an observation and isn't trying to be petty or mean, but it makes me bristle all the same.

"Why do you say that?" I ask, but it comes out a little harsher than I intend.

"He just doesn't seem to care about his job all that much."

I sigh loudly, making Mark shift a little. He's not much for confrontations.

"Want to walk again?" he asks. I shrug. I was thinking that a walk around the park would be better than staying in my room and reading the letter from my parents again, but I'm beginning to have second thoughts. We walk in silence for a few minutes, passing the quartet performing in front of the barbershop and the Gibson Girl Ice Cream Parlor. Mark stops in the shade of a tree.

"My father used to bring me here when I was little," he says, pointing at the store in front of us. "Of course, that was when it was the House of Magic and not the Main Street Athletic Shop." We watch as a man comes out of the shop carrying two baseball caps and leading a crying boy. "There was this magician who used to do his act outside."

I think about not answering, but realize I'm being nasty to Mark for no reason. "Like the disappearing ball and the taking coins out of kids' ears?" I ask.

"Exactly." Mark smiles at me. Confrontation averted. "He'd do the same tricks every time we came, but I never got tired of watching him. My favorite one was when he'd make flowers grow from a cone of paper." I turn and look at Mark. Somehow, hearing him talk about when he was young makes me really look at him for the first time. There's something in his eyes that is so genuine, so *there*, that it's sometimes hard to look at. Like at any moment someone is going to come along and try to take that away from him. I take another sip of my lemonade, draining the cup. Mark keeps looking at the front of the shop. "There was just something about it, you know," he says, looking over at me. "He made it look so real."

"Sometimes it's hard to tell what's real and what's not," I say, stirring the ice with my straw. I look up at Mark to find him staring at me.

"But it was just a trick," he says. "It was just spring flowers all folded together and secured with a rubber band."

"But you *thought* it was real."

"No. He made it look real. I mean, the trick was in a book that they had for sale inside." He tilts his head at me as if he's trying to see past whatever is blocking his way. "It was the illusion that was magic."

"But what if there wasn't a book, and all you had to go on was what you saw? What if you didn't even *know* it was a trick? Didn't know it was an illusion?"

"Ella, I'm not sure what you're asking." I can tell that he's trying to figure it out, but it's like he's trying to figure out what I'm saying when I can only speak Russian and he only knows English.

"I guess I'm just asking how you know what's real."

"The same way you know everything else," he says.

"That's what I was afraid of." He keeps watching me, but I look up at him and smile. "Want to walk some more?" I ask, and he smiles and takes my hand. Behind us I can hear

Winnie the Pooh and Rabbit start up again. Another performance. Another audience. Another show.

Aunt Sara said she would forward anything that came for me, but until today all I'd gotten was something from the alumni association at Vermont College addressed to "The Parents of Eleanor G. McKenzie," outlining the various ways they could stay involved in "the life of your college freshman." The letter in the blue envelope is on official Whole Heart Inspired Missionaries (WHIM—as in my parents decided to go halfway around the world on one) stationery and was signed by someone named Judith Reynolds. It outlines the various ways that I, too, can contribute to their organization. For just three dollars and ninety-nine cents a week (less than the cost of a glow-in-the-dark necklace or a pair of mouse ears), I can buy enough food to feed a whole village for a year. Different levels of contributions entitle me to different gifts. For a fifty-dollar contribution I get a WHIM mug. A hundred-dollar contribution would get me a WHIM T-shirt to wear to bed. I wonder as I refold the letter and slip it back into its envelope what gift my contribution of two parents entitles me to.

I feel bad about the way I treated Mark. Half picking fights with him and half asking him questions without real answers. He kissed me again before leaving me to go and meet up with Cassie to get to work on their list. "She's really eager to get going," he told me, letting his hand slide down my arm.

"I'll bet," I said.

"You aren't jealous, are you?" He leaned down to give me a kiss on the nose. *How cute, the princess is jealous.* And something inside me jumped a little, but it wasn't really jealousy, but more protectiveness. Something about Mark and Cassie together made me think of those inspirational calendars with a lamb sleeping peacefully with a lion.

"Just be careful," I said, reaching up for his cheek. I knew Cassie was just into Mark for his knowledge of all things Disney. Mark, with his earnest looks, was so trustworthy. I just didn't want to see Cassie gobble him up. So I let him kiss me again, making myself think about it. *Lip, tongue, lip, lip, fingers, cheek, lip, lip.* But I couldn't get past the biology of it, the anatomical description of it. I tried to think about it less, letting myself drift in the kiss, but that didn't work, either. I just ended up thinking about how damn hot it was even in the shade and how after all that lemonade I needed to get upstairs fast. And it wasn't because I didn't like the kissing. I did, but something about it just made me feel like I was holding my breath, waiting for something. Like if I tried hard enough, it could be right, feel right, but there was this little quiet voice that kept saying that it wouldn't. That no matter how many times we kissed or hugged or touched, it would feel exactly like this.

"Same time tonight?" I asked, more to make him stop kissing me than anything. He nodded and smiled before turning to head over to the other side of the park, where

I'm sure Cassie was tapping her foot and staring at her black Timex.

I lean back against my pillow and will myself to take a nap, but I can't get the image of the magician out of my head. Rabbits tumble out of hats. Flowers grow in thin air. Coins appear behind ears, and cards fly by themselves. There's a knock on my door, and I push myself to standing.

"Did you get stood up?" I call through the door before opening it to see Luke standing there.

"Stood up by who?" he asks, smiling at me. "Want to get to work on our list?" he asks.

"Only if you answer one question," I say, turning to push my feet back into my flip-flops.

"Depends on what it is," he says. I step into the hall and pull my door closed behind me. "Wait," he says, putting his hand on my arm. "I'll answer it."

"Okay," I say, sliding my sunglasses down over my eyes. "Luke S. Krause, do you believe in magic?"

Luke

After a day and a half of searching, we find the drawing of Mickey shaped like a piece of broccoli, and that same afternoon we track down the Bluebeard tomb outside the Haunted Mansion.

"We are kicking ass," I say. "And the broccoli Mickey is the only vegetable-related thing on the whole list. Unless you count Pinocchio, who's vegetable, I guess, in the sense of animal, vegetable, or mineral, since he's made of—"

"Would you *hush*," Ella says. "I'm trying to take a picture." We lean our heads together by the tomb and she holds the camera at arm's length and clicks it. When we look at the screen, most of my head is cut off.

"Nice job," I tell her.

"It's Bluebeard's memorial," she says. "Head-cutting-off

is appropriate." We delete that photo and try three more before one finally works.

"Well, that's two," I say, scanning our list. I glance at my watch; we only have an hour until we have to be back in costume. "Maybe we should look more tonight, after closing."

"I think we have dates," she says. We both sit, shoulder to shoulder, leaning against the tomb. At least it's in the shade.

"I think we don't," I tell her. "Cassie's feeding Matt intravenous coffee and NoDoz until their list is finished."

"It's Mark," she says. "You do that on purpose."

"No, he really is forgettable."

She elbows me. "I think Bluebeard is a little racy for Disney, you know? I mean, what with the serial killing of spouses and all."

"Yeah, but the colorful beard makes it seem fun. You know, whimsical."

"Was he even real? Did he exist?" She yanks the list from my hand and looks over it, drawing her finger down the page.

"Matt? No, he was just a bad dream. It's all okay now."

She tries not to laugh. "God, you are such an ass. You remind me sometimes—"

She stops like someone has slapped her, the smile vanishing from her face. She looks away for a moment, almost like she is talking to herself.

"Of?" I say. "Ella, what's wrong?"

She swallows. "Nothing." She shakes her head, smiles like

someone is holding a gun on her and telling her to smile. "You just remind me of a multitude of other asses I've known. It's hard to choose." She studies our list like it suddenly contains the secrets of the universe. I watch the side of her face for a minute, wondering what it can be, what's in there creating a sadness she is scared even to acknowledge.

"Anyway," I say, "the answer to your question is no." I click the button on the camera, looking back over the pictures we've taken, thinking how much I like seeing us together in them.

"That was the have-you-ever-met-anyone-cooler-than-me question, right?" She stands and holds her hand out to yank me up.

"Not quite," I say. Her hand might as well be electrified, sending currents and waves all through me.

"Oh, then it was the have-you-conquered-the-bed-wetting-issue question. Thanks for your honesty." She laughs out loud as she slaps the dirt off the back of her shorts.

"Be glad *smart-ass* isn't on our list," I tell her. "Everyone would be coming up to take pictures with you." We walk off toward Frontierland, where we figure to find "whiskey bottle," number 127 on the list. We could probably just look under Robin Hood's bunk, but Frontierland sounds like more fun, with fewer smelly socks.

"Everyone already *does* take their picture with me, silly," she says.

"Well, I guess a healthy ego is a good thing."

"Luke, I'm *Cinderella*, remember? I'm like photo central."

I nod. "Yeah, I forget that. Not too many people are clamoring for pics of Dale." We stop at one of the kiosks, trying to figure out how to get to Frontierland.

"I bet Chip is," she says. "Naked ones, even. Then she'll sell them for a profit, invest, and you can both retire at twenty-one."

I ignore the little dig at Cassie, the way she ignored mine at Mark. Actually, since all of this started, I spend my time with Ella pretty much pretending that Cassie doesn't exist, but then when I see Cassie, she smiles at me, kisses me, and I feel guilty, like I abandoned her. She pulls me in close to her and whispers that she missed me, and when I really look at her, I realize I missed her, too. Beautiful Cassie. But the weird thing is that it feels like I miss her more when she is standing there holding me than when she is gone all day. So I hold her tighter and close my eyes, smelling her hair, and she will make a little sound in her throat, and I hold on to those things, the little sounds, her smells, thinking they might be enough to fall in love with. Is that how it works for everyone? But all the while some part of me is wondering if I will open my eyes and find her not there at all, my arms embracing nothing.

"Well," I say to Ella, "*all* the photos of Dale are naked, since he doesn't wear any clothes, so I don't think there's that big a demand."

She briefly takes my wrist to tug me down an asphalt path to our left. Electric currents again.

"Yeah, what is *up* with that?" she says.

"With what?" We move past groups of people, whole families, and I notice how many of them seem just worn-out with too much heat and too much mandatory enjoyment. They always look like they've been mugged, forced by vandals to have a nice day.

Ella tugs me again, and for half a second I think I feel her hand linger on my wrist. But no, it's just me, some kind of wish. And despite what it says on all the information kiosks, wishes don't always come true.

"Okay," she says when the crowds thin out a little, "what is the deal with Disney pants? I mean, the most obvious example is Donald Duck. He wears a sailor shirt, so he has some combined sense of fashion and modesty—but no pants? If you had to choose, shirt or pants, what would you leave the house without?"

"I understand your position," I say, as though we are two philosophers arguing phenomenology, "but you're missing the larger point—that I'm not a duck. Your question is moot, professor."

She tries hard not to smile as she continues. "Yes, point taken. But Donald is anthropomorphized to have human, not duck, qualities. I mean, he speaks, he's married, he has anger issues, and so on."

We pass through the upward-pointing sharpened logs that indicate a Wild West fort, and suddenly we are in Frontierland, crossing over this little bridge across a pond. In the middle of the bridge, kids are buying food out of a gumball machine to feed to the fish.

"Why would they put a goldfish pond in a fort?" I say.

"Hush, we're discussing cartoon clothing, remember?"

"Or the lack thereof."

"Exactly." She points to a strip of grass that rings the pond, and we settle in beneath the droopy branches of a willow. Crowds are still moving about all around us, but it feels like we are inside something, inside the tree, hidden. And safe, I think.

"Well, think about this," I say. "Mickey sometimes has pants and no shirt, sometimes a tuxedo, magician's robe—"

"His closet is full," she says, settling beside me against the trunk of the tree.

"Exactly," I say. "But Winnie the Pooh? Same as Donald, shirt and no pants. For most Pooh characters, total nudity— except Christopher Robin, but why not him? He's no more or less human than the rest."

"It's like there are no rules," she says, nodding.

"And you know what else? Goofy wears pants and shirt and vest and hat, and he's a *dog*. Goofy can speak and drive a car; yet Pluto is *also* a dog, and he wears nothing but a collar and he barks. I mean, my God, it's chaos."

"Well, listen," she says, "you know how we established

that Donald spends his life pantless? Then tell me, please, why whenever he gets out of the shower and wraps a towel around his waist, he blushes when it falls down? I mean, it seems like inconsistent blushing to me."

I start laughing, and she bumps me with her shoulder, cutting her eyes at me.

I bump her back, and she bumps me, and then we stop and she is leaning against me, her brown shoulder pressed against the sleeve of my T-shirt.

"Maybe we should forget the list," I say. "I mean, we get three hours off and we spend it running around the park? Seems dumb when our job is to run around the park."

"Yeah." She picks up a blade of grass and uses it to poke my leg, then tosses it away. She seems suddenly very far off again, like there is some movie playing deep inside her mind and she keeps stopping to watch it. She pulls another blade of grass and shows it to me.

"What?" I say.

"I think it's the only real thing in the park," she says. "Nothing else, just this."

"You're in the park," I say, taking the grass from her fingers and using it to tickle her forearm. "I am, too. We're real."

"Nah," she says, shaking her head. "Not even close. We're a creation of the park. I'm a princess, remember? My life is perfect."

"You don't have to work here to play a part, Ella. Most people spend their whole lives doing that. I mean, you were in high school, right? Besides, it's not all bad, the unreal part."

"How do you mean?"

I watch the blade of grass move up and down along her arm, watch the goose bumps form under the pale hairs on her skin. "Well, like my reality, for example," I say. "Like Cass said the other day, big job, big truck, big money. I'm all set."

"And?"

"And that life seems as unreal to me as this place. It's the *same* as this place, you know? Spend your life in a costume saying what you're supposed to say."

"So what's real, then?"

I look at her, and her green eyes are looking right back at me. Really looking, like she is searching for something in my eyes, in my face.

"The thing you haven't imagined yet. The thing that's out there, that you have to go look for. The problem with this place . . . someone tried to package a dream so they could sell it. As soon as you package it, then it stops being a dream."

"So how does that figure into your life, all that stuff with your dad?"

I shrug, putting the blade of grass into her open hand. "You asked me if I believe in magic, and I said yes, and that's how. You just step out, start pulling your life out of the air. You make friends, you find work you really like doing, you find places. You find diners and Laundromats. You find beaches. You find a junk car and drive it for a month, then leave it beside the road. You find someone to fall in love with you. You make it all up as you go. Or, you know, maybe it makes you up."

"But what about your dad?" She looks suddenly like she can barely breathe. "Luke, what about what was *supposed* to happen?" As she says it her eyes rim up with tears.

"Ella, if it's magic, then nothing is *supposed* to happen. And everything is. You can't pick and choose. My dad chose for me, and it's like some trick where you can see the wires and the mirrors and the hole cut in the floor. You know it's fake all along."

She nods. "Yeah, but what if you find something you really love, and it disappears? That's magic, too, right?"

"Yeah, I think so. If you want the real magic, you take your chances. If you want the fake kind, stay here and smile at everything."

She looks out through the branches of our tree, out at Frontierland, where right now Davy Crockett and Pinocchio are sitting on a bench in the sun sharing a hot dog. It's a funny sight, and she does smile, the movement of her mouth making her eyes finally spill over. Her tears land on the pale skin of her forearm, rolling down toward the blade of grass, which curls in the middle of her palm.

After dinner Cassie finds me in the bathroom we all share, standing in front of the mirror in shorts and T-shirt drying my hair. One thing about this job, you end up taking about five showers a day.

"You missed dinner," I say. "And you can guess what Mr. Forrester is going to say about Blank and Dale. I think you need to be there."

"So, how'd you guys do today?" She stands behind me and slips her hand around me, up under my shirt.

"We got two. And I mean it, Cass. I felt kinda stupid out there dancing with myself."

"Is that what they call it now, Billy Idol?"

"Cass . . ."

"Okay, Mr. Bossy, calm down." She plants a row of tiny kisses along the back of my neck. "Wait," she says, pulling back a bit. "You got *two*? Like, two columns, you mean, right?"

"No. Two as in two. Two things. But they were really *good* ones. We're going for quality over quantity."

She smiles at me in the mirror, over my shoulder, her hair down and falling across her eyes. But I can see something else in her face, too, something sharp.

"You are sooo lame, baby," she whispers in my ear, then briefly bites my earlobe. "Ask me how many we found."

"How many?" I ask as her hand travels up the middle of my chest.

"A hundred and twelve. It's amazing. I mean, I have the organization, like what order to move around in, and Mark . . . well, what's there to say? It's like touring the forest with a squirrel."

"The chipmunk and the squirrel," I say. "Pretty hot."

"What are you, jealous? What were you doing all afternoon, finding *two* things? What were you up to?"

"We were just talking, Cass. And you made the teams, not me."

She turns me around to face her, and I see all over again how gorgeous she is, her hair down and loose, her eyes bright blue and alive. Really, she looks like someone from a magazine.

"I think you need to be talking to me, not her." She slides her hands over my shoulders, her blue T-shirt lifting up over her tanned belly as she raises her arms.

"You weren't here."

"Is that how it works, Luke?" Her gaze falls away from my face for a moment, and she looks genuinely hurt. "You can only see what's in front of you? Would you like me to be like that?"

I look at her, shake my head. "No, I wouldn't."

"I mean, I talk to Mark, but I'm not *talking* to him. I'm thinking about you, about us."

About winning, I think, but don't say it. How can I? I mean, she's right—I shouldn't be here kissing Cassie when all I thought about all afternoon was kissing Ella. That's not how I want it to be, not any of it. If the world is fake, then I don't want to be fake, too.

"You're right," I tell her, letting my fingers move through the tips of her hair.

She smiles and slips her hand around my neck to kiss me. "Ooh, say that again," she says, smiling as she presses her mouth to mine. We kiss, and then she moves her mouth beside my ear, whispering to me.

"Baby," she says, "I spent the day with that dork for *us*. I am going to get us that night alone, I promise." She reaches down for my wrist and pulls my hand up, outside the folds of her T-shirt, until my fingers are resting on the curve of her breast. "You think about that tomorrow when you're out moving around the park, okay?"

I nod, but can't really speak, can't move, my fingers just lightly touching her. She kisses my neck a final time, tells me she has to meet Mark, and, as she exits the bathroom, looks back at me one last time, smiling like she's already won.

At midnight I tell myself I'm just going for a walk or that maybe Cass will be there to meet me near the castle again, but some other part of me knows the truth, and knows it more fully when I see Ella sitting in the shadows, on our old bench. It seems now like years ago, those nights we used to sit out here and just talk. Or the night she walked off holding hands with Mark. It's a pretty chilly night for Florida, and she's wearing flannel pants with pictures of sushi all over them and a Red Sox T-shirt, playing her usual game of kicking off her flip-flop, then sliding it back on.

"When you're right, you're right," she says. "Totally stood up."

"Hey, you don't win corporate promotional contests by lying around on your butt sleeping all night."

"Gandhi said that, right?"

"I think it was Mrs. Gandhi. She was kinda pushy."

"Like someone else I know." She scoots over to let me sit.

"Looks like we're going to win," I say, letting her comment slide.

"Yeah, at our pace . . . we *could* win if the contest was extended until, say, the next millennium."

"No, ding-dong, I meant we are going to win by default. We get the prize and don't have to do a damn thing."

She nods, looking off. "Hurrah," she says.

"I know."

We are quiet a few minutes, until she starts smiling to herself. "I had fun today," she says. "I'm still laughing about the pants."

I smile back at her, nudge her knee with mine. "I'm thinking Dale needs some gym socks and a farm cap."

She laughs. "You know, they originally had an eighth dwarf, who didn't have pants, and his name was Sleazy."

"Yeah, right."

"No, for real. The animators drew him into the movie, then had to take him out."

"There's no way," I say. "I don't know where you heard that, but there is just no way."

"I have it on good authority. Mark told me when I told him about that stuff we were talking about today. And he should know."

I feel like I've been punched in the gut, all the air forced out of me. I thought our time under the tree was just that— *our* time, not to be shared with others. Then again, why wouldn't she? Suddenly, I'm feeling like an idiot.

"Well," I say, "I'm shocked."

She looks at me and smiles. "I know. I mean what were they thinking?"

"No, it's not that," I tell her, almost trying to pull back my words as I say them. "I'm shocked that Mark would talk to you about anything that involves pants. He seems a little . . . delicate for that."

Her smile disappears; her face looks flushed, even in the dim light. "Mark isn't *gay* or something, Luke. He's a gentleman, not climbing all over me at the breakfast table like your girlfriend does. He's nice to me. He's nice."

"'Nice,'" I say. "That sounds really thrilling."

"He can kiss," she says quickly, not looking at me, her eyes wet. "He's a good kisser, Luke. That help you get the picture?"

"Yeah, that's great," I say, feeling like I want to sink into the bench, into the concrete beneath the bench. "Not as good as Cassie, I bet."

"God, you are such a child. I mean, nice retaliation."

I look down at my own feet, shaking my head. "It's only retaliation if it hits, Ella. You don't care what I say about Cassie. You just don't like her, that's all."

"Well, Luke," she says as she stands up to leave, "wrong again. I hope Cassie will be a little nicer to you. Enjoy your prize. And by the way . . . yeah, it hit. Right on target. Congratulations." She turns and walks off into the dark, toward the dorm, and it's all I can do not to jump up and follow her.

Ella

Some things just suck by default, like a rainy day when you're planning a picnic, or getting the flu when you have sweet tickets to a Sox game. But other things suck in a way that you don't expect. Like you're just rolling along enjoying your day, your weekend, your life, and WHAM, out of the blue, major suckage. And not just the crap-I-stepped-in-gum kind of bad, but the hits-you-like-a-meteor-from-outer-space bad, and suddenly you can't breathe or think or even remember anything before that very moment. I've had three moments like that in my life. The first was when Ash died. That was the worst. Like the Hale-Bopp comet just slid out of its trajectory and smashed down hard on the edge of Maine, tipping it into the ocean. The second was when my parents bailed and suddenly I was floating, not like a kid's balloon drifting into the sky, but like one of those giant ones from the Thanksgiving Day Parade in New York City. Like instead of being held down by a hundred volunteers dressed as elves, Snoopy is sliding up into the sky, faster and faster, until he's just a speck in the clouds, and the TV anchors are babbling on about where it might finally make landfall and kids are crying and the head elf is being dressed down by some upper management at Macy's. I felt like Snoopy that day, looking down on what used to be my world.

The third sucky moment was today. And it wasn't just a moment, but a string of minor bad moments all strung together, so that they make a chain that threatens to wrap itself around my neck and strangle me. And the thing is, when I look back over today and try to tease out the various moments, I know the real answer as to why I can't breathe can't be found in just today but instead over the last year. Like Ash's death was a train engine and all these cars kept getting hooked to it, sliding along the rails, going faster and faster until there wasn't any hope of stopping it. If I look closely, I can see the cars. The orange tank car of my parents heading off to Africa. The green boxcar of leaving my house and my friends to come down to Florida, where instead of fall, they have cruise season, and to celebrate summer, they go inside and live in the air-conditioning for five months. There's the yellow hopper car of my aunt's house, where I practically raised her kids for four months while she got pedicures and facials and went to Botox parties. The purple boxcar of coming here and realizing that once again, I don't quite fit in. Like everyone has the life manual and all I got was the CliffsNotes version, which gives you the major plot points but tends to skip over the important details.

It's the blue gondola car hooked on the back that surprises me. At first, I was just mad, hearing my flip-flops slap against the soles of my feet as I walked away into the darkness, the noise hitting the buildings all around me and echoing into the night. As if I give a damn about how Cassie kisses. I stop in front of the banner advertising Cinderellabration, inviting guests to JOIN THE HAPPIEST CELEBRATION ON EARTH. "Not bloody likely," I whisper to the cartoon image of Cinderella beaming out at me. I keep walking past the entrance to Fantasyland and into Adventureland. I walk up the steps to the Swiss Family Robinson Treehouse, ducking behind a tangle of vines when I see the light of a flashlight bobbing in the dark. I sit against the base of the tree and wait for the guard to pass. Getting caught by security and receiving a lecture from Evelyn isn't how I want to spend the rest of the evening.

It's funny how even when it's just you in your head, you try to pretend like nothing's wrong. Like everything is just fine, thanks for asking. It's not like I've never thought about Luke that way—in the more-than-just-friends way. I mean, he's smart and funny, and the look in his eyes when he thinks he's just gotten one over on me almost makes me want to fall into them, but that's the thing that stops me—the desire for that falling and the knowledge that sometimes when you let yourself fall, you just end up splattered across the rocks.

The flashlight beam bounces off the acacia tree in front of me, making me squeeze farther back into the shadows. The rough bark pulls at my hair as I look up into the branches of the tree. If I concentrate hard enough, I can almost imagine that I'm sitting on an island out in the middle of the ocean waiting for a ship to come and rescue me. Maybe that's the real problem. I keep waiting for someone to come along and take my hand and tell me it's okay and they'll help me find my way back home. But it'll never happen.

A giggle from the other side of the fence makes me sit up and look over at the flashlight. Not a security guard at all. Two shapes are outlined against the log fence that separates the Tree House from the Lost Boys Campground. Another giggle, and then a low voice and more laughter, this time quieter. I push myself back to standing and peer into the darkness. The spill of the light actually makes it harder to see their faces than if they were in the dark, too. All I can see are two pairs of legs, one ending in pink flip-flops, the other in deck shoes. I step forward toward the railing, hoping to see under the low branches, but the snap of a stick under my foot makes them shut off their light. I hold my breath, counting silently in my head, waiting for them to move forward again.

"Just the wind," the low voice says, but the light doesn't come back on. I back up into the shadows again, this time wedging myself between two bunches of hanging vines.

"Are you sure it's up here?" the other voice asks. This one I recognize—Cassie. Then I hear the flutter of pages. The list. The other voice is Mark's.

"Just around the bend in the stairs," he says, ducking his head under the closest branch. "Careful," he says, and I see him reaching back for Cassie's hand to help her step across a chain designed to keep visitors off the grass. I lose sight of them as they walk under the stairs and up to the trunk of the tree. "See?" Mark says. "You can see the outline of his ears here and here." I imagine him tracing his finger along the bark, drawing the outline of a mouse over the wood.

"Okay," Cassie says. "Ready?" A sharp flash of light from under the stairs. A giggle again, this one fainter. More intimate. They step out from under the stairs, Cassie clutching at the back of Mark's shirt. They stand in the middle of the sidewalk, blinking against the darkness, then start to walk toward Peter Pan's Flight, slowly, letting their eyes readjust to the night. Cassie places her hand in the middle of Mark's back, as if to steady herself. "I can't see anything," she says, her voice soft.

"Me neither," Mark says, smiling over his shoulder at her.

I sit back down on the wooden steps and lean back against the tree trunk, tilting my face up toward the upper branches again. *It's funny,* I think. *Neither can I.*

Ash and I didn't fight. I mean, sure, in the who-gets-the-last-Toll-House-cookie way, but not in the big I'm-going-to-kill-you way that I've seen in the park, where brothers and sisters look like they would gladly trade each other for one of those character-shaped juice boxes if they could. I think it might be partly because we were so close in age—only a little over a year apart. Also partly because he was a boy and I'm a girl. No clothes or Barbies to fight over. But I think the real reason we got along so well was the fact that from the day I was born, our father told us that we *had* to get along. There wasn't a choice involved. If Ash got invited to a birthday party, so did I. If I had skate night with my friends, Ash could come along. He was my best friend—even when I was eight and I crashed his secret scout campout, making it so he had to walk me home in the dark while everyone else got to tell ghost stories and eat s'mores. And even when he was a senior and I sprayed his car with shaving cream for graduation and the cream accidentally started eating away at his paint job before we could get it all washed off. Even when I went with my parents down to Yale for Parents' Weekend and I got food poisoning from warm potato salad at the picnic and ended up puking on his roommate's bed.

Ash was always the smart one. The one who could always make me laugh. The one all my girlfriends had crushes on. It's safe to say I practically worshipped him. That's not to say he didn't have faults. He was a slob. He couldn't make a peanut butter and jam sandwich without making the whole kitchen sticky. He was often hard to read—off in his own world, his own head, barely there. I sometimes wonder if that was why he had the accident. If maybe he was think-ing about an exam he just took or about a girl he just met, or even just dreaming about nothing in particular. Letting himself drift as he slid along the dark forest road until a deer jumped out or an icy spot hooked his wheel and his car flipped clear off the road and down the slight rise before it came to rest at the base of an old pine tree.

The police officer told my parents that he died instantly, that he didn't feel a thing, but I suspect they tell everyone that. They say it was about half an hour before another car drove along that same bit of road, the back way from Ellsworth to Machias. That it was another twenty minutes before the volunteer firemen from Cherryfield could get to the site of the accident and cut a hole through the side of the car so they could pull Ash free from the wreck. I hope it was like that—instantaneous. That he didn't have to sit there and slowly fade away, because I know what he would have been thinking about then. I know while lying there in the cold darkness, drifting, he would have been thinking about me.

"Do you know who speaks Elvish?" Amy spears a kiwi wedge with her fork.

"Need a translator?" I ask. I'm trying to stuff breakfast into me and leave before I run into Luke or Mark or Cassie.

"It was on one of the cards," she says around her bite of kiwi. "I'm thinking Robin Hood."

"You know you're either going to have to reopen the

game or burn those cards, don't you?" I take another bite of oatmeal.

"I like knowing everyone's secrets," Amy says, spearing another bite of fruit, a strawberry this time.

"It's not like you know who they all belong to."

"Some. The rest I'm working on."

I take a sip of my coffee and look up as the door opens again. A couple of the Merry Men walk in.

"You done?" I ask, pointing to Amy's plate, which is still half-full. She squints at me, but when I don't say anything, she just nods. We walk over to the plastic tubs along the back wall. One for scraps. One for silverware. One for plates and mugs. We go out into the courtyard. Early in the morning is the only time it's even half-pleasant out. Beside me Amy munches on an apple she took out of her sweatshirt pocket.

"You're not supposed to take food out of the cafeteria," I say, heading toward the picnic table under the trees. "I think that's rule number seven."

"You obviously didn't read the memo with the cafeteria rule addenda," she says, climbing on top of the table and resting her feet on the seat. "It said that portable food could be taken out of the cafeteria in an emergency." I sit beside her and pull my sunglasses out of the kangaroo pocket of my sweatshirt and put them on.

"Is this an emergency?" I ask.

"You tell me." We watch a seagull pick at the remains of what looks to be a slice of pizza.

"It's complicated," I say, resting my palms on the table and leaning back.

"Love always is." She pitches her apple core toward the trash can. It misses, bouncing into the grass. Her voice is soft, almost carried away by the breeze. "Ella, let me ask you something." She turns to look over her shoulder at me, and I nod. She looks forward again, watching the seagull peck at the apple core, trying to free its seeds. "If you had a choice to make between doing something safe and doing something that could either make you really happy or completely blow up in your face, what would you do?"

I watch the seagull try to fly with the core in its beak, dropping it each time it gets more than a few feet off the ground.

"I guess it depends."

"On what?"

"I'd do a cost analysis on it. You know, figure out what I would stand to gain versus what I would stand to lose."

"What if it's everything either way," Amy asks. "And it doesn't depend on you, but on something you can't control?"

"Sounds like a bad risk," I say. The seagull grabs at the core again, pressing it into the ground for leverage.

"Yeah," she says softly, resting her chin on her hand, making her bangs fall over her eyes. The seagull hops once, then twice, before rising into the air. He banks hard and flies over us, the apple core clutched tightly in his beak.

• • •

"How many?" I ask, fiddling with the clips on my earrings. I had to get new ones from the props department. The pearl-ized coating was starting to peel off the old ones, making it look like they had leprosy.

"I don't know," Mark says around a yawn. Besides the dark circles under his eyes, he's still as handsome as ever.

"Ballpark."

"A hundred." I raise my eyebrow. "Okay," he says, "maybe more. I don't know. Cassie's in charge of the list. Not me."

"What are you in charge of?" I ask. My voice sounds funny in my ears. All bumpy and pointed. I told myself last night and this morning that I wasn't jealous, but I can hear it in my voice.

"Ella, what's wrong? Didn't you sleep well?" Mark stifles another yawn, which makes his eyes water.

"Better than you, I guess." I fluff the sleeve of my dress, trying to keep from looking at him. I've decided to try harder, and maybe feeling jealous is part of that. *Mark is a good guy,* I tell myself. *He's polite and kind and pleasant and . . .* I try to think of another synonym for *nice,* but I can't.

"She's brutal. I wanted to stop at two, but she wanted to keep going."

"And what Cassie wants . . ."

Mark puts his hand on my arm, just above my elbow. I finally look at him, watching as he tries to swallow another yawn. I smile at him, and he smiles back.

"Hey, Cassie doesn't get this," he says, bending and kissing the side of my neck. The music on the stage changes as the mice push through the curtains and past where we are standing. "Don't be mad, please." He kisses me again, letting his lips brush the top of my shoulder. "I told you I was sorry about last night. The time just got away from us."

"I'm not mad," I say, turning to face him. And it's true. I'm not. At least not anymore. He bends down to kiss me again—on the mouth this time. His lips are soft and warm and slightly sweet from the lemon drop he just finished. "Mmmm," I say, my lips still brushing his. It's an act, like the one we are about to do for thousands of people. Only this one is just for Mark, and maybe for me. I keep telling myself that if I just keep floating along, no one will get hurt. I'll do my time here, and when they finally resolve the strike, I'll head back up north again. If I keep kissing him and letting myself be kissed, it will look like a love story. The music changes again, and Mark takes my hand.

"You ready?" he asks.

"As I'll ever be," I say. But saying it aloud scares me. What if it's true? That all this safe fantasy and pretend magic is all I can handle? What happens if your make-believe turns into make-do? Mark pushes aside the curtain for me, and I step out onto the stage and into the sunlight. A banner flutters in the breeze near the side of the stage. WHERE DREAMS COME TRUE . . . and I wonder if that's right. Are they *your* dreams that come true, or someone else's? Dreams that are packaged and advertised and sold by a marketing team so good that you begin to believe they *are* your dreams and they actually have come true. Mark slides his hand around my elbow and leads me up the steps toward the waiting throne. The crowd grows quieter as we near the top. Mark steps forward and takes the crown from one of the footmen. He lifts the crown over my head and pauses for a moment as the audience applauds. This is where it happens. This is where the dream factory chugs away day and night, making you want only the things you can buy off a shelf and take home with you. Mark places the crown on my head and the music starts and the crowd claps and the mice dance. Here is where they tell you, if you only believe, you, too, can live happily ever after.

Luke

The first thing I think is, *I have to tell Amy.*

For a minute I can't think of his character name—Foulweather? Foulmouth? Actually, that would be pretty funny. J. Worthington Foulmouth, and all his animated movies are rated R. But no, as soon as I say *that* to myself, I remember . . . Foulfellow. His costume is unmistakable—a giant fur fox head that looks about ten times heavier than my Dale head, a big green top hat, cape, cane, spats—all of it just the way Mark described. I'm thinking, too, that he must be on break because he's sitting on the ground with his back against a palm tree, and he's eating a plate of nachos. The weird thing is the way he slips a nacho, dripping melty cheese, up under his fur head and, I assume, into his mouth, but it doesn't really look like that. The move is so deft that

I can't even see the character head move, and it pretty much looks like one of Pinocchio's friends is just hanging out and eating nachos. I can't see how he does it. I mean, all this week Cassie and I are supposed to give out these rubber pencil toppers of Chip and Dale, only I can never pick up the little Dales when I'm wearing the fur hands, no matter how hard I try. I end up just reaching into the bag and scattering them on the ground, and Mr. Forrester has already yelled at me for it twice. "The pencil toppers are not birdseed," he told me. Of course, sitting around and eating nachos is also a mortal sin in the Church of Mr. Forrester, but what's he going to say? The guy is on *break*, trying to have lunch, and still he's greeting little kids, shaking hands, posing for pics, all of it. A true believer.

The only reason I'm in Fantasyland in the first place is because I got a note from Ella that morning saying it was probably better if we just split the rest of the list and work separately and that I could have *O* thru *Z*. I start with an easy one, Tinker Bell, and after I forget about J. Worthington Foulfellow and his nacho trick, I find about a million Tinker Bells in the gift shop: Tinker Bell key chains and wallets and rubber stamp kits. And as soon as I pick one up and hold it in front of me and hold the camera out and point it at myself, I remember Evelyn's first rule—we are competing in pairs. Siamese twin pairs, not distantly orbiting stars pairs. Damn. For half a minute I even have the stupid idea to find some substitute, some thin brunette girl, maybe wearing sunglasses, who would pose next to me and smile, and if the picture were cut off or blurry enough, it would be good enough to fool everyone. I'm also wondering if we are really distant stars in orbit, and right now Ella is in some similar gift shop holding a Buzz Lightyear doll, looking around for someone who looks like me.

But it's not because of the contest, not even close. It has been two days now, and Ella won't even look at me. I walk into breakfast and she just keeps scraping her spoon in the bottom of her oatmeal bowl like she wants to tunnel her way through. I've gone as far in my head as to wish she would be all over Mark because I know somehow that would be for my benefit, but there is none of that. And then I hope she will sit far away from me, like even negative attention is still attention, but there is none of that, either. This morning she sat right across from me, and I said, "Good morning, Ella," more like it was a question, which I guess it really was, and she just glanced up, looked at me, gave a half smile—an elevator smile—and went back to eating.

I look around the store one more time, still standing there like a moron, holding the camera and the Tinker Bell doll, and spot several young brown-haired women, some of them with sunglasses. At the same time I totally give up on the idea, for one simple reason—there is no one else like her.

Back outside, before heading back for the after-lunch parade, I take a few minutes to watch J. Worthington Foulfellow finish the last of his nachos. It's not until he stands that I can see in him the age that Amy described. He moves like an old man, a little slow to get up, using his prop cane, stretching his back after he does so. Some phantom he is, I think. Then again, maybe if you are stuck long enough— in your costume, in your past—you really do become a phantom, some slippery shadow of yourself, haunting your own life.

On the way back I work my way through the crowds, from the Peter Pan pavilion all the way over to Cinderella Carousel, and there he is *again*—J. Worthington Foulfellow, shaking hands, walking with his brass cane, posing for pictures. For half a second I'm thinking that Amy is right, because I *just* left him standing beside the tree and there's no way he passed me and I didn't see it. He's just *here*, from out of nowhere. I walk over near him, notice the little smear of nacho cheese on his white glove, and when he walks past me, I touch his sleeve and he stops.

"How did you get here?" I say.

He starts to do the whole pantomime—putting his hands on the sides of his head, exaggerated shrugging—the things we were taught to do when we're at a loss, like the time a Japanese tourist group asked me where to find Elvis.

"Okay, stop," I tell him, making sure to speak into the eye vents. "I *work* here, as Dale. How did you get here?"

He marches off to the side into the trees, still in character, motioning me to follow him.

"You're a scab, aren't you, kid?" he says, his voice muffled, rough, a smoker's voice.

"We all are—except you."

"I don't get your question," he says. I can nearly see him through the mesh, a pucker of wrinkles around his eye, a shock of white hair hanging wet across his forehead.

"You were at Peter Pan, ten seconds later you're here. What gives?" I hold my breath, half expecting him to just vanish suddenly.

"Utilidors," he says, a word that sounds vaguely familiar, like some Spanish phrase I may have once learned. I shake my head.

"The utility corridors," he says, impatient. "God, you newbies don't know shit. What are they teaching you in orientation?"

I shrug. "No drugs. No groping. That's about it."

He clucks his tongue, and I wish more than anything he would take off his head to talk to me; but of course, there is no way he will. Rule number one. "Yeah, the short version. You aren't exactly here for the duration, are you?" he says. "Strike is going to be settled any day now." I wonder if that's true. Every day the picketing crowds outside the gates grow larger.

"Why didn't you strike?"

He shrugs. "My job. I have never missed a day. Not once

in thirty-three years. Anyway, you use the tunnels, kid. Nine acres of them, under the park. That's how we move around. Think about it—you ever see a delivery truck here? An ambulance? A plumber? The bread man? Don't you think we have all those things? All underground, where you are supposed to be when you walk over to the parade or the campfire or what have you."

"Why?"

He uses his white-gloved hand to rap me on the head. "You think some little kid wants to see Chip and Dale walking around with the Seven Dwarfs? See Minnie eating lunch with Snow White? How confusing would that be? Use your damn head, kid." He shakes his giant fox head sadly. "They aren't teaching you guys a damn thing, are they?"

"I guess not."

"It's easy." He points beside us, a pink door next to the restrooms marked AUTHORIZED PERSONNEL ONLY. "You go in the pink door, down the steps, head south. You'll see a bunch of wires and crap, hoses, peat moss, what have you, and it'll look like a parking garage under there. Keep walking, see more steps, look for a purple door, and that's Tomorrowland. Brown is Frontierland, and so on. Piece of cake."

"Cool," I say. "Thanks."

"Don't mention it, kid," he says. "You need a Band-Aid? A rake? A stretcher? Duct tape? It's all down there. Just remember—anything real is hidden."

• • •

The next afternoon we're given an ice-cream social in honor of Cinderellabration, which is only a week away, and we inexplicably have it outside the Enchanted Tiki Room, sitting on the lawn listening to the mechanical toucans squawk. At least there's some shade, though eating ice cream in the Florida sun is not the best idea, it turns out. People end up more or less drinking their sundaes and banana splits, while Anna and Robin Hood explore some of the erotic possibilities of chocolate syrup. Jesse hangs out with the other Merry Men while they joke about cherries and make half-hearted attempts at food fights, and every five minutes or so, he goes and sits by Amy, who is leaning against one of the totem poles, looking like the lowest and saddest of all the carved faces. We hardly ever see management types anymore—Estrogen, Bill Tubbs, Mr. Forrester—they all seem to be missing in action, and I wonder if J. Worthington Foulfellow is right about settling the strike. The idea of it gives me a stomachache, going back to the world that's waiting for me, leaving things the way they are with Ella forever. Then again, things can stay that way forever even if they *never* settle the strike. She barely looks at me anymore. The weird thing is, she barely looks at Mark, either, and they are totally a couple now. It's not even enough effort to make me feel jealous. When he walks into the cafeteria, she doesn't even notice he's there until he walks up and kisses the back of her neck, and when he leaves with Cassie, she doesn't even watch him go. She smiles when he talks, listens to him, holds his hand, but there's something empty about it. She holds his hand like someone else said, Here, hold this, like you would hold a can of Pepsi or something.

Robin Hood looks up from spooning ice cream into Anna's mouth. "Hey," he says, "how come Cinderella gets her own celebration?"

Ella blushes, smiles. "Maybe I deserve it?" she says.

"Yeah, but Robin Hood steals from the rich," he says. "That's cool."

"And he gives to the . . . what do you call them?" Anna says. "The unrich."

I'm happy to see Ella briefly cut her eyes at me, to see me react.

"The unrich *and* the poor," I say.

"Exactly," Anna says, and even Robin Hood looks a little embarrassed.

Cassie and Mark are nowhere around, off winning the contest. Some of the Merry Men have even tried to beat them by cheating, all of them wearing identical Atlanta Braves hats down low over their faces for the pictures so that they can have three teams out at once, the pictures interchangeable, and they are still getting their butts kicked by Mark and Cassie.

Last night I got back to the dorm after she did, even

though we did a Chip and Dale Campfire together on the beach and some little four-year-old kid wanted me to explain to him, while he was crying, why we weren't allowed to have an actual campfire and instead have a fake fire, one of those orange-lit, wavy fabric things. And even though we aren't supposed to talk, I learned that comforting a four-year-old with hand gestures is damn near impossible, and so I spoke, gave him the whole Smokey the Chipmunk routine about fire safety, just making it up. When I finally did get back, Cassie was gone with Mark again, but she had propped up one of the brochures for the Old Key West Resort on my pillow, along with a perfumed note on pink paper, written in her small, neat writing, telling me how soon those two nights will be ours and how it will be a memory that will last us forever. And I knew what she meant by it, knew how sweet it was, how romantic, and I knew, too, that Robin Hood and Jesse would think that note was a gift from God, but somehow when I read it and read it again, I just couldn't breathe. And not in a good way, either. We would have those nights, and I would take her home to meet my family, and she would charm them, and she'd be with me on holidays and take me home with her, and the whole time I would just be going along with all of it, going along like the little kids at the Tomorrowland Indy Speedway racing around think-ing they're driving, steering those cars around the track, but the whole time the cars are just on rails, and there's only one direction they can go.

"You know what we need?" Robin Hood says. "Robin Hood-abration. I am kind of the unsung hero of the whole enterprise."

Jesse leans back in his chair and laughs. "Well, I bet Anna there already has a few Robin Hood abrasions," he says, making the other Merry Men and the Army Men laugh.

Suddenly Amy stands and throws her plastic banana-split boat against the totem pole, so that bits of banana and ice cream soup go everywhere. "God, you are so *gross*," she says, practically yelling it. Ella and I cut our eyes at each other. Amy stomps across the grass and stands in front of Jesse. "You don't always, *always* have to worry about impressing those assholes, you know? Maybe you ought to worry about impressing someone who's worth it." She looks around like she's searching for something to throw at him, but all she can find is the plastic spoon she's been holding the whole time, and that she just drops in his lap. Then she leaves, out past the Country Bear Jamboree, and gone. Ella tries to follow her out but comes back a minute later, shaking her head.

"That was random," Robin Hood says.

Jesse makes a couple of halfhearted attempts to play it off, but I can tell he's shaken up, hardly looking at anyone.

"You know what we *really* need?" I say, trying to slice through some of the embarrassment. "We need . . . *Dalebration*! with an exclamation point."

"Well, the exclamation point is what makes the whole thing work," Ella says when no one else takes me up on it.

"Hey, you might have something there, Krause," Robin Hood says. "Celebrate all the second bananas." Anna briefly looks into her banana-split boat before figuring out that's not what he's talking about.

"Hell, yeah," Jesse says, looking relieved to be off the hook. "Chip gets all the glory, gets top billing. Screw Chip."

"I *wish*," Robin Hood says, then looks at me. "Sorry, dude. But Jesse is right on. I mean, are ya'll pickin' up what he's puttin' down? Man, let's celebrate Brer Fox, and Governor Radcliffe, and Liver Lips, and Launchpad McQuack, and Max, and . . . you know, *all* the losers." He looks at me again. "Sorry, dude."

Ella leans forward, waving her hands. "Yeah, *yeah*," she says, "and we can have like those off-brand sodas from the grocery store, like, you know, when they name them Dr. Perky, and Mr. Aaah, and Southern Lightning. And like 'fig bar cookies' instead of Fig Newtons, and—"

"And generic beer," Jesse says.

"Wow," I say, "you guys are making me feel like crap." But the party is planned, the party to celebrate everything forgotten and second-rate. But Ella is looking at me for the first time in days, and she's smiling, and that, by itself, is enough to celebrate.

It's probably after one in the morning when I hear Mark come into the dorm room, and by the third time he trips over something and then shushes himself, I figure out that he's been drinking.

"Mark, what are you doing?" I say in a loud whisper.

"We," he says, then hesitates. I see him in the dim light pointing theatrically to his own chest. "We have all but won the contest."

"No *way*," I say, but he misses the sarcasm.

"Yes," he says. "Sad but true. We *almost* won, and she kissed me."

I lean up on my elbow as Mark sits and tugs off his sneakers, so that they skitter across the floor, and someone, one of the Army Men, tells him to shut the hell up. I'm just thinking that I'm not sure which of his statements interests me most, because I know it ought to be the second, but really, it's the first. If Mark were Robin Hood, I might be a little more worried. "What do you mean, almost won?" I say.

He shakes his head, tugs at his sock. "We have maybe seventy-five things left. That's like *nothing*."

"Yeah, that's like ten minutes for you guys."

He succeeds with his sock and sits there holding it. "Except there's all this crap, like five things, and we worked on those, and *nothing*. No thing."

"Like what?"

"Like a garden hose. Oh, and like PVC pipe? What is that, anyway?"

"Plastic pipe," I tell him.

"Oh," he says, and nods. "We can't find it. I mean, we looked everywhere."

Utilidors, I think. Both those things are underground, in

the tunnels. But how can Mark, the reincarnation of Walt Disney, *not* know about the tunnels?

Mark leans back on his bed, still wearing one sock. "Do you think, Luke, that maybe they're talking about some kind of *magic* garden hose? I mean, you think?" And there is my answer—Mark doesn't know about the tunnels, because he doesn't *want* to know about the tunnels. He is the truest of the True Believers. Cassie, on the other hand, just doesn't know.

"Yes, Mark, that's what I think. And if you keep looking and, most of all, keep believing, one day you will find that magic garden hose."

He is quiet.

"And listen," I say, "what do you mean she kissed you? Like a little kiss because you are almost done, a celebration?" I think back to earlier, our plans for Dalebration. Maybe Cass is planning her own celebration. I think that, try to see it, and my stomach knots up once—a small, hard knot of jealousy—but just as quickly unravels itself. Mark, having heard from me the story of the magic garden hose, is fast asleep.

Maybe an hour later, in the middle of a deep sleep, I feel someone pushing my shoulder, and right away I know it's Mark, about to get sick after his first-ever bout of drinking. But it turns out I'm wrong.

It's Ella.

"Get your butt up," she says, "and follow me."

I grab a pair of shorts to slip on over my boxers, plus a T-shirt and sneakers, unlaced, and before I can manage any of it, she is walking out the door and down the steps in her Red Sox sweatshirt and sushi pajama pants. When I make it outside, finally, I find her at the usual spot, sitting on our old bench, where we haven't sat since the night I watched her walk off into the dark.

"Okay, listen, you," she says.

"Hey, your boyfriend just came in drunk. And I think we can win this contest."

She hugs her knees up to herself. "Do we care?"

I sit beside her. "About which?"

She shrugs. "Either?"

"I guess not."

"Well, then," she says, and turns to face me. "I have a question for you."

"Okay," I say, and nod, holding my breath, thinking in half my brain how pretty she is, her hair pulled back, her cheeks dusted with freckles.

"What is your middle name?" She slightly twists her fingers together, nervous, breathless, waiting for me to answer. And instead of thinking about why she might be asking, I just open my mouth and tell her.

"Skywalker," I say.

She blinks. "Your name is Luke Skywalker?"

"No. My name is Luke Skywalker Krause."

She half laughs, and for some reason her eyes rim up with tears. She seems really, genuinely happy. "You just, like, *told* me," she says.

"Well, you asked." I smile at her.

"Okay, Luke. *Everybody* asks."

I nod. "Let me try that again." I clear my throat. "Well, *you* asked."

She puts her hand on my arm. "Wait, wait—you have a brother, Ben . . ."

"Kenobi. Yep," I say, and she laughs again.

"I don't know where to start. How about this? You know, it's an . . . unusual name, but it's not creepy or anything, so why do you keep it a secret?"

I think about this one for a few, not really looking at her, not really knowing where to look. I watch her hand, which is still resting on my arm.

"I don't know. See, my parents named me that, named Ben that, because back in the day they were like these total *Star Wars* freaks." I look up at her. "They went to all the conventions, and right now, stuck away in a shoe box, are autographs from Mark Hamill and Carrie Fisher. They had this *Star Wars* wedding at one of the conventions, and my dad was dressed like Han Solo; my mother, like Princess Leia. The best man was a Wookiee."

She laughs. "Then he was just best Wookiee, right?"

"I guess."

"Why does it make you sad?"

I shrug. "Maybe . . . I don't know. It's like they gave up. Like they did all that because they really liked it and it was cool, and then suddenly they 'grew out of it,' and were all ashamed of it, treating it like everything they'd done had been stupid. It was *their* idea that I just tell everyone my name is Luke S. Krause, not mine."

"Maybe they did grow out of it. People grow out of things."

"I get that, but why are they so ashamed of it now? Why can't your life just be what it's going to be, instead of what it's supposed to be?"

"So this is about you right now, not twenty years ago, yes?"

"I don't want to give my kid a name and then make him hide it. I don't want to say, Be this, not this. I don't want to be locked into being someone who locks other people into the same thing."

"That almost made sense." She smiles at me. "Listen, if you don't want to be that, then don't."

I look at her and shrug. "It scares me. I think it's like saying, If you don't want to have size eleven feet, then don't. You're kinda born into it. Or you inherit it. And then . . . whatever you're handed, you're stuck with it. Forever. You wake up, and that thing is your life."

She gets really quiet then, looking away from me, and I suddenly feel stupid, knowing there is a sadness in her that's way deeper than being stuck with an oddball name. I want her to tell me; I want to ask, but the moment feels as fragile as a soap bubble, and I just sit, letting her touch my arm, afraid to even breathe. Finally, as if there never had been a lull in the conversation, she looks at me, her eyes rimming full.

"God," she whispers, "I hope that's not true."

Ella

Someone should make up a list of rules for visiting amusement parks. Every day I see the same mistakes, most of them totally avoidable. For instance:

1. You should never wear any item of clothing that matches an item of clothing that another family member is wearing. That means no couples with matching tracksuits and visors. No small children with identical Mickey Mouse T-shirts, and no families sporting orange T-shirts emblazoned with FIFTH ANNUAL ELLISON FAMILY REUNION.
2. You should only visit a theme park with either an overdeveloped sense of irony or none at all. Either way you'll have fun.

3. Under no circumstances should you ever wear anything resembling a fanny pack. Whoever thought up the idea of wearing a pouch that sits above your bum and holds your money and keys and parking stub should have his or her clothing designer license revoked. These flatter no one.

4. Never allow your travel agent to talk you into the Behind the Scenes Tour. All you end up seeing is exactly that. The servicemen fixing the power panel that controls the Dumbo ride. The vendors carting around juice boxes to all the venues. The sanitation engineers cleaning up after someone barfs on the Magic Carpet Ride.

5. Don't buy the refillable plastic cup thinking you're going to save money in the long run. What are you supposed to do with the cup while you're riding the rides and seeing the shows? Besides, once you've carried it around for half the day, resting it on the floor of the Splash Mountain ride, you really don't want to drink out of it, anyway.

6. The final rule, and this might be the most important one, the one that everyone seems to forget: Don't put too much pressure on your Disney visit. It's still you there. You with all of your problems and issues. You and your reality in the midst of all that fantasy. Don't expect the Magic Kingdom to be, well, magical.

· · ·

"Give me a bite of your hot dog, you will." I don't look at Luke when I say it, but out of the corner of my eye, I can see him smiling at me.

"Okay, Yoda, the Jedi mind trick only works on weak-minded people."

"You will give me a sip of your Coke," I say. He laughs and passes the cup to me. We've pretty much given up on our list. Instead we're using the camera to capture what we refer to as Disney Moments. Those little scenes that never make it to the tricolor brochures or onto the official Disney websites. So far today, we have a photo of a man dropping three double-dip cones in the trash when his preschooler threw a fit because he didn't want mint chocolate chip, but chocolate chip. Luke got a shot of J. Worthington Foulfel-low attempting to scratch himself through his fur crotch. I took three pictures, one right after the other, of a little girl barfing into the flowers after the Pirates of the Caribbean ride made her cotton candy go sour.

"Ten bucks says the guy in the purple Chucks starts freak-ing out." Luke holds the camera out in front of him, center-ing the couple in front of us in the viewfinder.

"I'm not taking that bet," I say, taking a long drink of the Coke. "They've been circling each other for ten minutes now."

"Any second now." He adjusts the camera a bit, and I hear the whine of the zoom. "Wait for it. Wait for it."

"Luke, you do know this is sick, right?"

"I'm not doing anything. I'm just documenting events."
We watch as the man starts talking loudly, waving his arms.

"They got married at the castle yesterday. She even dressed
up as Cinderella. Talk about setting your sights a little low."
She starts yelling, too, and the surprising thing is no one
even looks at them when they pass. Luke puts the camera
back on the bench, beside him.

"Did you hear about the strike?" he asks. I shake my head,
and he looks at me. I feel the knot in my stomach that grows
each time the strike is mentioned. Luke takes a sip of his
Coke, pulling on the straw until it makes a loud burbling
noise.

"Luke, the strike?"

"They're stopping talks until after the final night celebration. Management's decision."

"How come you're suddenly in the know?"

"When have I been out of it? I mean, of the know."

"The dumb is strong in this one," I say. Luke shoves my
knee with his hand, then leaves it there for a moment, his
palm burning into my skin.

"Foulfellow told me, and he stanks of the know."

I squint at him, and he grins. "I guess that's good news,"
I say. "But there's a window, you know? I want the strike to
continue until I need to leave for school, but not beyond
that." As I talk, I can hear my voice getting softer, like I'm
trying to hide what I'm about to say next. "I mean, we can't

stay here forever." Luke stops smiling and looks away from me and toward the entrance to Tomorrowland.

"Do you ever wish you could see way into your future? Like twenty, thirty years from now? See what you're like?"

"Like if you're bald or something?" I ask, but it's the wrong thing, because he won't look at me. I pull my legs up into my chest, letting the backs of my flip-flops hook onto the seat of the bench.

"Or something," he says, but so softly, it's almost drowned out by the newlyweds arguing.

"Luke, I can barely see past today. Barely handle what's happening right now. I don't think I want to know what I'm like in twenty or thirty years." I take the cup and shake some of the ice into my mouth.

"But what if seeing yourself could make you change who you are now? What if making one tiny change now could ripple through the rest of your life, making bigger and bigger circles until everything is different?"

"I don't know," I say, looking over at the entrance to Tomorrowland, the city of tomorrow looking suspiciously like old episodes of *The Jetsons*. "If I had to look at every decision like it was going to have major repercussions down the line, I wouldn't even be able to choose between wheat and white toast for breakfast."

"Rye."

"Why what?"

"Not *why*. Rye. Rye toast."

"*Eww*, you can't put raspberry jam on rye toast."

"Rye not?" Luke laughs, pushing my leg again, and again leaving his hand on my knee. "It's just that my family, my father, has these plans. Plans that have been in place for longer than I can remember."

"And you're not sure you want them to be your plans." Luke just shakes his head. "Well, what do you want to do instead?" He shrugs and looks at me, then at his hand on my knee, then back at my face.

"I don't know. See, that's the thing. I don't have a better idea or even another idea, really."

"Well, find one."

"What if it's the wrong one?" He moves his hand from my leg and reaches for the camera again.

"Then change it."

"Just like that?"

"Why not?" I can still feel each of his fingers on my leg, feel where it's almost too cool now without the heat of his hand.

"You can't just change your plans. You have to set a goal and then work toward that goal." He lifts the camera. This time aiming it at me.

"Says who?" I ask, suddenly self-conscious with him watching me.

"My father."

I put the cup over my mouth and breathe loudly into it. "Luke," I say, making my voice deep, "I am not your father." I hear the whir of the camera taking a picture and stop mid-breath. "Oh, great. I'm sure that's a nice one. Here," I say, reaching for the camera. "Let me see it." I aim the camera at him, finding his face in the screen. "Okay," I say. "Do something."

"Like what?" He tilts his head and looks right at the camera. Right at me.

"Anything," I say, holding it still.

"Anything," he says softly. I push the button and the shutter clicks. *Anything.*

"I just went for a walk." Amy leans over the railing of the bridge and watches the koi swimming in the pond. "It's weird that they have real fish here. You'd think they'd have robot fish or something."

"At Disney we don't call them robots. We refer to them as *animatronics*. And you're changing the subject." I lean over, too, and watch the bright orange one, my favorite, swim under the bridge and disappear from sight.

"I just got upset is all. Don't you get sick of those assholes with all their double entendres, like they're the stars of their own cable show?"

"They've been like that all summer." The orange fish swims back into view and does a hard turn to the right, following a black-and-white marbled one. "You get a bunch of eighteen-, nineteen-year-old boys in a room with too much time and that's what happens. I mean, that's a pretty big generalization; but for the most part, it's true."

"Maybe," she says, twisting a strand of her hair around and around her finger until it looks like it's wrapped in gold ribbon. "Ella, do you think it's possible to like someone before you even really know them?"

"Like who?" The two fish zip by again, the orange one in the lead this time.

"Theoretically."

"As in, I have this friend who has this friend who has this friend who might possibly like someone?" I say.

"Okay, Ms. Holmes, you have seen through my artful ruse." A family walks onto the bridge, stomping their feet on the planking and scaring the fish back into the shadows.

"Are you asking me if I believe in intuition? Like if you can know something without really being able to explain why?" The breeze blows around us, shifting the water, so that it's harder to see through it.

"I guess," she says. "Has that ever happened to you? Have you ever really been drawn to something or someone without any real reason?" I keep watching the water as if I'm going to find an answer spelled out in the ripples. The truth is, I have felt that . . . maybe am even still feeling that.

"Maybe," I say. "I mean, it's tricky, you know?"

"Tricky how?"

"I think it's easy to confuse intuition with wanting something." I'm trying hard to keep this about Amy, but tiny bits of me keep poking through.

"But what if it isn't something you wanted, or looked for, or even imagined? And what if it pulls at something so deep inside you that you didn't even know it was there?"

"I think it can be dangerous." The fish are beginning to slip back out of the shadows, the sunlight making their scales flash as they swim. "I mean, what if all of that is true? What if you have found something big and real and profound, and you open yourself up to it—then *wham.*"

Amy turns and looks directly at me. "Wham?"

"Yeah, like what if suddenly that thing that you've been floating on, holding on to, and falling into is suddenly just gone?" She tilts her head at me, and we are both quiet. Both listening to the splash of the water as the koi nip at the gnats hovering just over the surface.

"I don't know, Ella," Amy says, leaning back over the handrail. "Even if that is true. Even if all you get is a glimpse of that big thing or you just get to hold it for a second, I think it's better than not having it at all."

"Maybe," I say. The orange fish is chasing the black-and-white one again.

"What if someone told you that you could have one piece of the very best chocolate in the whole world?"

"How big of a piece are we talking here?" I ask.

Amy just shakes her head, but she's smiling. "Not big. One bite. But you have a choice. You can either have that one piece of chocolate with the possibility that you could have a lot more or you can have a lifetime supply of Oreo cookies."

"Gross. But what are the odds that I'll get more of the really good chocolate?"

"You don't know. No one knows." The wind blows again, harder this time, and the water ripples, so that the fish disappear. "We'd better get going," she says. "We're going to get soaked." I look up at the sky, watching the clouds that are forming over the castle, changing it from fairy castle to scary haunted castle.

"I told Luke we'd meet him at the Morocco pavilion at four," I say, checking my watch. Cinderella's arms point to four and eleven. A gift from Mark. "We still have about five minutes."

"Are you thirsty?" Amy asks.

"I'll buy you a sweet lassi from the Indian market."

"Mango?" she asks.

I make a *pfft*ing noise with my lips. "As if there's another kind."

"Well, there's plain."

"Blasphemy." We start walking past Fantasyland and toward the gates that will take us to the Epcot monorail.

She laughs. "The church is getting pretty strict if not adding fruit to a yogurt drink is considered an affront to God."

"I take my beverages very seriously." I watch the shadows disappear as the clouds move over us. "Are you excited to meet this Foulfellow guy?" We walk toward the faux marble buildings and the tented booths that are supposed to mimic a Moroccan street fair.

"I just can't get my mind around working here for thirty-three years."

"As a fur character."

"As anything," Amy says. We walk under a series of awnings toward India Star.

"Apparently he lives here, too."

"In one of those houses at Bay Lake?" The rain is starting, making soft noises as it hits the canvas canopy. "I thought only Disney elite got to live there."

"Luke said Foulfellow used to live there, but it got too crowded for him." We make it to the front of the line, and Amy orders two mango lassis—large.

"There're only eight houses. How crowded could it be?" she asks, turning to look at me.

"Okay, Amy. This is a guy who has worked all of his adult life as an evil fox who wears a top hat and white gloves." We take our lassis over to a table on the edge of the food court.

"Point taken. So." Amy takes a sip of her drink. "What's the deal with Luke?"

"The deal?" Without wanting to, I feel myself blushing, my cheeks turning pink.

Amy looks at me for a long moment, taking another pull on her straw. "I meant him and Foulfellow."

"Oh, I guess they're friends. Sort of."

"Kinda like ya'll are friends?" Amy asks, and I can feel her watching me. Watching as my blush deepens. I try to think of something to say when I feel a poke between my shoulder blades. "Luke," Amy says, still watching me. "We were just talking about you."

"Good things?" he asks. He pulls out the chair next to me and sits down. "Ella, give me a drink of that, you will," he says, stretching out his legs.

"I feel strangely like I should give you a sip of this," I say, starting to pass him the cup and smiling.

"Weak mind," he says.

"Then again." I pull the cup back and put it on the table in front of me.

"Please?"

I look over at Amy. She's chewing slightly on her straw and watching us.

Luke takes a sip of my lassi. "I'm glad you got mango."

"You like mango?" Amy asks.

"As if there's another kind," Luke says. "I mean, *plain*? Please. That's a culinary tragedy."

"That's pretty strong language," Amy says, still watching my face.

"I take my beverages very seriously," he says. "What?" he asks, seeing her smiling at me. "I do."

I feel myself getting warm again, feel my cheeks get hot, but this time it doesn't stop with my face. I feel the warmth spreading into my chest and stomach and spilling down my legs.

"So what do you say?" Luke says. "Should we get going? Foulfellow's place is over on the other side of the park, but I know a shortcut."

"You are in the know," I say, pushing back from the table.

"I am," he says. "I mean, in the know."

I can't stop laughing as we head out into the rain. It's cold on my skin, but it doesn't touch the warmth that keeps spreading and washing through me.

Luke

The living room of Foulfellow's trailer is pretty much the whole thing, other than a kitchenette, as he calls it, and a small bathroom, and a bedroom with a pile of dirty clothes shoved in one corner. The whole place looks like a museum exhibit called something like *American Life: The 1970s* because everywhere you look, it's dark paneling, and orange shag carpet, and avocado appliances in the kitchenette, and an eight-track stereo system up on a bookshelf on the wall, with a shoe box of tapes (all the paper covers wrinkled) by bands like the Bee Gees and the Electric Light Orchestra. Foulfellow keeps running around straightening things, shoving copies of *Playboy* and *National Geographic* under the couch, which is decorated with scenes of covered wagons and horses, the middle cushion sagging badly. By now, after having lunch with him three or four times and helping him last week to move a new TV into this place (which he just set on top of the old, broken TV), I am pretty much used to seeing him without his costume; but I can't, no matter how hard I try, get used to his name. He repeats it now, shaking hands with Amy and Ella.

"Name's Bernard," he says. "Bernard Fitzgerald Laurant, which is Cajun French, except for the Fitzgerald part, which I like to think of was me being named for Kennedy, you know. The president? Of course, that's impossible, at my age and all." He wipes his mouth with his fingers, but little white flecks remain at the corners of his mouth. I get the feeling we are the first real visitors he's had here in . . . God knows. Twenty-five years it could be. I keep trying to peg his age, but the best I can do is older than parents, younger than grandparents. *Bernard*, I tell myself again. *Bernard, Bernard.*

Amy and Ella shake his hand and introduce themselves and take nervous little glances around the place, at all the orange shag and paneling. Now that I get a good look at the place, there are some details I hadn't noticed last week, like the strips of flypaper next to the front door; or the frozen dinner trays in the trash; or the piece of string across the kitchenette, where he has hung up coffee filters with clothespins, I guess so he can use them again; or the back wall that's covered with old Disney bumper stickers. Some are from way back, like the faded one that says DISNEY, IT'S A WHOLE

New World! from when the park first opened, and some are newer, Got Mickey?, and some just weird, like the one that has a picture of Eeyore and reads Talk to the Ass! That one, I'm betting, isn't official.

"So," he says, "you kids like working here?" We are all just standing in a cramped circle around his coffee table, which is filled with pieces of jigsaw puzzle, some of them spilled on the carpet, mixed in with spilled potato chips. We nod and say it's okay, it's not bad except for the heat, and suddenly, I'm wondering if this whole visit is a mistake. I mean, why did we come here? Just to look at him?

Finally, he tells us to sit, sit, and we all do, the three of us squeezed in on the wagon-train couch while he sits across from us in a faded blue recliner, and then just as quickly jumps up to get us something to drink, saying all he has is tequila and tomato juice and root beer. And water, he says, but no ice. His gray hair is standing up in crazy cowlicks, like he just got out of the shower and brushed it with his fingers, and he's wearing a Ron Jon surf T-shirt and Dickies work pants and Wal-Mart sneakers with Velcro instead of laces. I've noticed this, how much more nervous he seems without his J. Worthington Foulfellow getup, as if all the smart-ass remarks, all the "hey kid" stuff and his raps on the head are things he puts on with his costume.

"So," Amy says, once we all get our tomato juice in jelly jars, "thirty-three years, huh?"

He nods. "Yessir, thirty-four if you count the six months

I worked garbage detail. Let me tell you, garbage can bring this place to its knees."

I can feel that none of us has a clue what that means, so Amy just keeps asking questions. "So," she says again, "I guess you have seen a lot of changes around here."

He nods and sips his tequila. "Yes," he says.

Ella is quiet sitting next to me, but she nudges me with her knee, signaling . . . something.

"Well," Amy says, "do you have any examples?"

He looks worried for a second, and the longer we sit there, the more agitated I feel, almost like it's hard to keep sitting. I look around the room, collecting details of it—the bottles of rubber cement sitting next to a pile of ragged sneakers, the dusty Niagara Falls needlepoint hanging on the wall, the magnetic poetry kit on the fridge, a framed photo of a woman on a beach in some old skirted bathing suit and rhinestone sunglasses, the computer on the floor behind the recliner with a bald eagle screen saver. His whole life is in the place. *Life in a can*, I think, like it's something sold in a convenience store.

Bernard is still thinking, then he starts nodding so fast, he spills some of his drink. I feel Ella's knee pressing into mine. "Yes—hey, you kids will get a kick out of this one." He smiles, his teeth large and whiter than I have ever seen, so much so that I decide they must be fake. "Back in seventy-one, right after the park opens, the big thing is Tomorrowland, right?" He looks at all three of us until we nod, confirming this. "Well, get this. One of the main attractions of Tomorrowland is called—" He starts laughing so hard he can hardly get the words out. "It's called *Flight to the Moon*. Can you believe it?" He shakes his head, still laughing, his face red. "Flight to the freaking moon," he says again, rocking back and forth a little.

Ella and Amy and I cut our eyes at each other, and Amy gives a slight shrug. "Wow," Ella finally says, her voice uncertain, "what were they thinking?"

Bernard looks at us. "Well, you get it, right? I mean, this is 1971. The first moon flight had been *two years earlier*. I mean, what's that, Yesterdayland?" At this he cracks himself up laughing, so that he's bending forward. Amy and Ella look at me like all of this is my fault, but Ella can't keep herself from smiling.

"Bernard?" she says. "You are so nice to have us over. Can I ask you something?"

"Pretty girl like you? Ask me anything you like."

She nods. "Well, when you are here, and you come home from work, and you eat your dinner—what do you think about?"

I can hear the question inside her question: How do you get your thoughts around your life? How do you reconcile yourself to yourself? How do you make it make sense, finally? They are my questions, too, but I wonder what's making her ask them.

Bernard ponders for a while. "Well," he finally says, "I've

been thinking some about Billy and Benny McCrary. You know them? They were the world's fattest twins, back in the day, and they even played a gig here once, riding around on their tiny motorcycles."

Ella nods, nudges me again.

"I've seen a picture of them, I think," I say. "So . . . you just think about them in general?"

"No, no." Bernard shakes his head. "I'm thinking how Billy died first, a full ten years before Benny, and I'm wondering what Benny did. I mean, how did he bill himself? The world's fattest twin? You can't have one twin, right?"

Amy shrugs. "Maybe he was the world's fattest man after that."

"That's just the thing," Bernard says. "He wasn't. Not even close. So his brother dies, and suddenly he's not anything at all. It's like he just lost half of himself, and after that he's just another guy with a weight problem."

Ella suddenly looks very flushed, and she stands up, struggling a little to do so with the sagging couch. "I think we should get back," she says.

"So soon?" Bernard says. "I have more tomato juice."

She nods, not looking at anyone. "Yeah. We don't want to get busted."

We leave and walk along in silence until Amy says, "Pretty weird, but I like him." She thinks for a moment. "Actually," she says, "I can say the same of just about every friend I have."

"Thanks a lot," I say, and smile at her. I look to Ella, but she's not even listening, just looking at the ground, putting one foot in front of the other.

The next night Cassie is in a good mood and so am I, because we had this special birthday campfire for some spoiled little six-year-old whose father hired us just to lip-synch "Happy Birthday" and dance around and hand out the presents (how many six-year-olds get their own DVD players?). But the cool part was, when we finished, the father tipped us both fifty bucks. We aren't supposed to take tips, which is, like, number 583 on the list of things we aren't supposed to do but do anyway. So we're happy.

Cassie walks out of the shower room in a T-shirt and shorts, her hair just blow-dried, and slips her arms around me. "Save that money," she whispers. "I'll get Robin Hood to hook us up with some really good champagne for our nights at the Old Key West."

"Did his mead source dry up?" I say.

She blinks. "What?"

"Nothing," I say, and kiss her, my own hair still wet. "Dumb joke."

This feels like the first time I have seen her in a week, and I'm only seeing her now because Mark insisted on taking a night off because of the poison ivy he got while looking in the bushes for stuff from his list. ("It's not like he has poison ivy of the eyes," Cassie said when she first told me.)

"I'm glad you're here," I tell her, almost surprised to discover how much I mean it. I feel almost nostalgic for Cassie, if you can feel that way for someone you've known only a few weeks. Or maybe I'm just nostalgic for the days when I thought I could come here and forget all my problems. I remember our very first day at the park and how she sat next to me in orientation because she said at least I didn't look criminally insane, which is more than she could say for some others there, and how an hour later, over our first Disney lunch, she told me that she'd sat there really because she thought I was cute, and then she reached across the table and took my name tag, trading for hers, and we wore the wrong ones for the rest of the day, and I couldn't believe this amazingly beautiful girl was giving me this much attention. All day I wondered what it would be like to kiss her, to touch her blond hair. And so I touch her hair now, remembering, and it feels like the first time, lifting the soft strands and watching them fall between my fingers.

She kisses me, pressing against me. "I'm glad you're here, too," she says. "Have you been behaving yourself while I'm busy winning the contest for us?"

"Of course," I say, kissing her hair. I feel the warmth of embarrassment push through me, and right then I'm glad to have an excuse not to be looking at her. Then again, I tell myself, I haven't done anything wrong—I've just thought about Ella, let myself swim in thoughts of her. But you can't control your thoughts, can you?

"What have you been doing?"

I tell her how some of us went over to visit Bernard, about his trailer and the story about Tomorrowland and the tomato juice in jelly jars. "You have got to meet this guy," I tell her.

"Uh, no. I don't think so." She shakes her head, still holding me. Down the hall I hear the Merry Men laughing at something on TV.

"Why not?"

She leans back and looks at me, her hands on my waist. "Luke, sweetie, I'm a *girl*. That guy is, like, a pervert. There's one story that he almost got fired three times for 'groping incidents,' but they can't ditch him because he's Roy Disney's great-nephew or something."

"And you believe that?" We start walking downstairs. Cassie told me earlier that after all the marching around the park all week, she just wants to sit under a tree and rest her head against my shoulder.

She shrugs. "I didn't *not* believe it. And even if I don't, I just have no desire to be around people like that."

"People like that . . ."

She takes my hand, pulls me toward Main Street. "I'm not a snob, Luke. It's like hippies, right? People think they were so cool and uninhibited, but what were they really like? They wasted half their lives doing drugs, then figured out what they actually wanted was BMWs. The whole thing is stupid."

"Stupid how?"

"Stupid to romanticize failure." She tugs my hand, and we sit on top of a brick wall watching the sun sink down in the sky. "Everybody pretends that getting ahead is bad, having ambition is bad, right? If you live in a trailer, then you're doing your own thing. Right? Stupid. Take *anybody* who thinks that way and offer them the deal. They can have a ratty trailer and jelly jars and broken furniture and all the freedom they want for the rest of their lives. Freedom and used coffee filters. How many people are going to take that deal?"

"Not many," I say. "Pretty much no one."

"Exactly. I mean, even *you* guys. Why did you go over there? Just to kinda *look* at him, right? Like he's a freak show?"

"A little, I guess," I tell her, embarrassed at the truth of what she's saying, remembering when I thought the same thing myself. And then I think of my own parents—if they were the same as thirty years ago, still dressing up in tunics and light sabers, they would probably have groups of kids coming by to gawk at them, too.

"That's all I'm saying," Cassie says. "I don't want to see life as a freak show. Least of all *my* life." She curls into me, slipping her arm around me, and whispers, "It's not bad to want things, baby. For example . . . I want *you*." She moves her hand along my thigh, just the tips of her fingers. She kisses me then, and I kiss her back, still thinking about what she's just said.

She pulls back and looks at me. "Luke?" she says. "I know

I don't have to ask, but *you* wouldn't take that deal, would you?"

I glance into her blue eyes, the way they search my face, half hopeful, half testing, then look away. Part of me is trying to think of how Ella would answer that question, or how she would *ask* it. But Ella isn't here. After ten minutes with Bernard, she ran out, scared of something. Maybe she wouldn't see Bernard's life in that trailer as a coin flip, not a heads-or-tails that you have to call in the air. But that's how everyone treats things—parents, teachers, bosses—if your life is not one thing, it will be another thing. I know that must be right, know Cassie is right, but I keep trying to make one correction in my head: If your life is not one thing, it be can *anything*. How much do you gamble? Once I was in Mr. Forrester's office, in trouble for something else, and his desk calendar said "If You Fail to Plan, You Plan to Fail." Maybe that's all that happened to Bernard, and maybe that's what happens if you fall in love with some girl from Maine when you've never even been to Maine, a girl with something hidden so deeply inside of her that she may never let you see it. If it's a gamble, then I know everyone's money is on Cassie. She's the safe bet. The sure thing.

I look at her, really look at her, and she smiles. "No," I tell her. "I guess not."

The next day I go by Fantasyland on my break and have a chili dog with Bernard. Now I have the opposite problem—

when he's in costume, I have trouble thinking of his character name. Bernard the Fox doesn't sound so terrible. And I think the same thing I did the other night—after almost three and a half decades inside that costume, he seems more comfortable when he's wearing it than when he's not. His steps are more agile, more alive, his gestures more certain, is maybe the best way to think of it. More full, more confident. All the shyness of Bernard eaten up by mean old Foulfellow.

On my way back I feel a tap on my shoulder, which usually means a dad wanting a photo, except I'm not Dale right now, just me. It's Ella, also on break, though her hair is still swept up on top of her head (her Cinderella hair, she calls it). She's eating a funnel cake on a paper plate.

"Hey, listen," she says, falling into step beside me. "Amy and I thought maybe we could all go in together and take a dinner over to Bernard's. You know, like we can make him some mac-and-cheese and cut up some lettuce and do some slice and bake cookies. I mean, we have more stuff in that dorm kitchen than you realize—"

"Ella . . . maybe that's not such a good idea," I say.

"Why?" She takes a bite of the cake, then breaks off a piece to give to me.

"I dunno." I take a bite and chew. Funnel cake always tastes like the carnival when you're eight years old. "Maybe it's like we're a church, and he's our shut-in, our charity case."

"You just had lunch with him, ding-dong," she says.

"That's different."

"Because it didn't involve doing anything nice?" She licks powdered sugar off her finger. "Sorry to break it to you, buddy, but your company is nice all by itself, even if he did pay."

"'Nice,' huh? Next I'll catch poison ivy and turn into a prince."

"There are worse things than nice," she says, though her voice makes it sound like she's having trouble thinking of any. "Besides, I'm kinda changing your status as we speak."

"To?"

She throws her plate into a Mickey trash barrel. "I will keep you updated."

"Look, Ella," I say, "you were the one who ran out of there the other night, not me. I'm just saying that whole thing was a little weird, and maybe we don't need to go back."

She looks away. "I wanted to leave because I was uncomfortable for a minute. Big deal."

"That's my point. It's *not* comfortable. We're going there for bad reasons. I mean, what are we, his friends all of a sudden?"

"Man, this doesn't sound like you at all. Yes, all of a sudden. That's how it works, Luke. You know, like five weeks ago you didn't know me at all. Now, oh my God, all of a sudden we're *friends*."

I nod as we stop in front of the dorms. "Yeah . . . friends," I say. I look into her face, her eyes, the depths of her eyes, like I could fall into them and keep falling, and that would be enough. You could fall forever and never worry about where you land.

"What is your *problem*? First you are anti–mac and cheese, and now you're upset that we're friends?" She turns from me and shakes her head, and I want to say that no, I'm upset because it feels like with us it's just a starting place—Step One. Become Friends. And there are eight hundred steps left, or a thousand, or an infinite number, but we—she— will always be stuck at one.

Ella

"I can't believe they added in another meal." I stuff my hair back under my wig, still slightly damp from lunch. "And why don't they have a Disney Prince lunch?" Mark smiles up at me from where he's sitting eating his apple. "It would be way easier," I say. "Forget finger sandwiches and punch. Throw some hot wings on a plate and pass a bowl of popcorn around and call it a day."

"Football and a keg?" Amy asks. "For the dads," she says, seeing the horrified look on Mark's face.

"Exactly." I swap out my pink headband for a lavender one to match my dress. "Think sports bar with royalty."

"Except that in most sports bars, guys in tights would get the crap beat out of them," Amy says.

"So what is the deal?" I sit down by Mark, who offers me a bite of his apple.

"The deal?" he asks, wiping at the apple juice running down my chin.

"None of the stories would work without the princes," I tell him. "Snow White and Aurora would still be in comas. Cinderella would still be a peasant. Belle and Ariel would be unhappy and lonely. Jasmine would be married to an evil magician."

"Aladdin isn't a prince," Mark says.

"Still," I say, poking him in the thigh. "You see where I'm going here. What's the deal with little girls and princesses?"

"I think it's the whole ever-after thing," Amy says, stepping into her black ballet slippers. "Boys don't think like that. Boys want to be space rangers or archers or cowboys, or swing around the jungle on vines." Mark nods, taking another bite of his apple.

"Okay, but Tarzan has Jane and Buzz Lightyear has Jessie and Robin Hood has Maid Marian. Those are all love stories," I say.

"Only because they're trying to make them cross over so girls will like them, too," Amy says. "If their audience were just boys, they'd just blow more things up or have more sword fights." I look over at Mark, hoping Amy is wrong, but he's still nodding. I take the apple from him again and bite into it, chewing and thinking.

"See, they figured it out. All this Disney princesses thing. They don't even *need* the movies or the stories or the books," Amy says. "All they need is a princess. And if one princess is good, then three or four or seven is better."

"Love in the economy size." I look down at the apple core in my hand, and suddenly, I feel like crying.

"I'm so thirsty," Mark says, putting his hand on my knee. The same spot that Luke had his hand. "Can I get you anything?" he asks, squeezing my leg.

"Orange juice." I don't look up at him, afraid that if I look anyone directly in the eyes, I actually will start crying. "Please," I say. I keep staring at the core in my hand, trying to figure out what to do with it. Mark walks back from the snack table with two paper cups.

"They didn't have orange. I got you apple, but juice is juice, right?" He hands the cup to me and sits down again, putting his hand back on my knee.

"Right," I whisper. I look up and see Amy looking at me as she ties the ribbons on her bodice. I just shake my head at her, and she looks away.

When I was seven, I fell out of one of the apple trees at the back of the field behind our house. I wasn't that high up, maybe five feet off the ground. I probably could have just landed on my feet had my boot not gotten caught in one of the branches. I remember hanging there for a few seconds while my foot slowly pulled free from my boot, a little at a time. I could see everything upside down—our house resting on the clouds, Ash running toward me from where he was collecting apples around the base of one of the other trees, a couple of old blankets flapping on the clothesline. It seemed like I hung there forever; then suddenly, my foot pulled free from my rubber mud boot and I began falling. Still in slow motion. Still upside down. Cats always land on their feet. Something in their inner ear always tells them which way is up, which way they should twist, which way is safe. Not me. The doctor at the hospital said I was lucky when Ash told him what happened. I held Ash's free hand as they put the cast on his wrist. He'd hit his arm on a rock. The rock I would have hit my head on if he hadn't caught me under the shoulders, letting me fall against his chest.

"I'll give you a million dollars," Robin Hood says from the doorway.

"No, yuck," Amy says.

"Two million."

"I'm not doing your laundry."

"I didn't say *do* it. I said help me do it." He leans against the doorjamb, watching as Amy and I sort through the secret cards. "Wait, what's that one say?"

"I think there's something wrong with me," I read from the card in my hand.

"That's it?" he asks. "Man, those are lame. 'I think there's something wrong with me.' Who doesn't?"

"What's wrong with you?" I ask, leaning back against my bed.

"Oh no. I know how you two are. I'm not getting dragged into that conversation. Next thing I know, you'll be telling me my inner little boy needs love or asking me about my relationship with my father."

"Is that why you're with Anna? Because she's . . ." Amy looks at me for help.

"Uncomplicated?" I say.

"No, because she's hot. I mean, don't get me wrong, both of you are pretty smokin', too."

"So suave," Amy says, flipping two more cards.

"Want to know what I think?" I ask, leaning my head back against the bed. I don't bother looking over at him. "I think you're with her because she's safe. She doesn't challenge you." He's watching me, his arms folded, still leaning against the doorjamb. "I think you're with Anna because there's no chance you're going to fall in love with her."

"I think you may be right," he says, making Amy and me look at each other. "Don't act so surprised. You two walk around here like you're untouchable. Like the rest of us are somehow beneath you. Like we're too base or immature or oblivious, but the truth is, the two of you are just as clueless as the rest of us. We're just smart enough to know we don't know shit."

"Okay, smart guy," Amy says, tossing her stack of cards back into the Mickey hat. "Tell us, then. Tell us what we're missing."

"Oh no. Dr. Love's advice is not for free."

"Since when are you Dr. Love?" I ask, stacking my cards and dropping them back in the hat, too.

"Since now," he says, smirking at us. "Tell you what. You ladies help me with my laundry—"

"You mean *do* your laundry," Amy says.

"Semantics. Okay, you two *do* my laundry and I'll tell you."

"How do we know you're not just working us so that we'll do your laundry?" I ask, pushing myself off the floor and sitting on the edge of my bed.

"Ella, I say we do it. Who cares if it's all a scam. At minimum it will be entertaining." Amy pushes herself off the floor, too, and walks over to where Robin Hood is still standing in the doorway. "You have yourself a deal," she says. "But I'm not touching any of your dirty clothes with my hands. God knows what they have on them." We follow him up the stairs to the boys' floor, the sounds of loud music and laughter getting louder as we approach the landing.

"Careful," Robin Hood says, putting his arm out in front of Amy to stop her from going through the door. A Frisbee flies past, ricocheting off the walls. "Incoming," he yells down the hall. We step through the ongoing Frisbee golf game and into the room that he and Jesse share. "Give me two minutes to sort these." We look around, taking in the "beer-amid" that's grown by several layers since we'd been up here and the large purple stain in front of his dresser. "Kool-Aid," he says, seeing Amy eyeing it. "Don't ask."

"So," Amy says, looking over at the neater side of the room, "where's Jesse?"

"Lunch," he says, holding up a red-and-white striped polo shirt. "Lights or darks?" he asks me.

"Darks," I say, watching Amy's face. She keeps looking at Jesse's bed, its spread tucked in tightly, the pillow plumped, a folded pair of khakis and a button-down shirt and a tie lying across it. "So, what's with the tie?" I ask. Robin Hood looks over his shoulder, then back at the heap of laundry on his bed.

"He couldn't decide whether a collared shirt was okay or if he should wear a tie. I told him no tie. 'Relaxed and confident' is my motto."

"I thought 'Loud and vulgar' was your motto," I say.

"That, too."

"So, who's he having lunch with?" Amy says, her voice coming out much softer than before. Robin Hood looks over at her.

"Some chick in Epcot." He keeps watching the side of her face, then raises his eyebrow at me.

"Hey, this laundry thing has an expiration date," I say.

"Keep your panties on," he says. "Or then again, don't."

"Eww."

"Okay," he says, pushing the last items into the two duffel bags. "Done." Amy and I each lift a bag and head out into the hall, careful to watch for flying objects. "Hey, light starch on the shirts." We listen to his laughing as we walk back toward the stairwell.

"I'll light starch him," Amy says.

"You do know that doesn't make any sense," I say, letting the bag bump against the steps in front of me as we descend to the basement.

"Okay, how about this? I'd like to give him a good spin cycle."

"Nope, too sexual."

"Ironing?" she asks. I shake my head and pull the door to the laundry room open, and she follows me inside. "Okay, I'd like to pop him in the mouth."

"Better," I say, "although a little on the violent side." I hear a noise that sounds like a wasp, and Amy reaches into her pocket.

"It's my mom," she says, looking at her cell phone.

"Take it," I say.

"You sure?"

"You can switch to the dryer in half an hour." She smiles at me and pushes back through the door. I hear a faint "hello" on the other side and then a laugh. I focus on dumping the laundry into the two washers, trying not to think about the phone calls that Amy gets from her family nearly every day and the ones I get—never. I pour a scoop of soap over each of the loads and twist the dial to EXTRA SOILED and close the tops. I don't feel like going back to my room and trying not to listen to Amy talk with her family, so I head to the TV room. I drop into one of the chairs facing the television and begin flipping channels until I hear voices outside.

"I am so dead. I could kill her." I flip the television off and walk toward the sliding door leading out into the courtyard. I can see Luke there talking to Anna. "I can't believe she spaced this." He sees me and lifts one of his hands and smiles a little before looking back at Anna. "We are already on suspension because she blew it at the campfire two nights ago, showing up nearly half an hour late."

"Is everything okay?" I ask, shielding my eyes against the sun. Anna just smiles at me and says nothing.

"It's Cassie. She's not here. One guess where she is," he says.

"With Mark."

He nods and looks back at his watch. "We're supposed to be at the jamboree in ten minutes."

"What jamboree?" I ask, worrying that I missed something.

"It's just for fur characters. Something Estrogen dreamed up so that we wouldn't feel left out of the Cinderellabration festivities."

"As if," Anna says. I look at her for a moment and then back at Luke.

"I'll do it," I say.

"You'll do what?" Luke asks.

"I'll be Chip," I say. "I'm free until the parade." Luke tilts his head at me. "I mean, how hard could it be? Just wave a lot and make *I don't know* and *after you* gestures. I can totally handle it."

"Other than the fact that you've just managed to dismiss my current life's work, are you sure?" he says.

"Totally," I say.

"Yay," Anna says, and she actually claps her hands together cheerleader style.

"Well, come on, then," Luke says, taking my elbow. "Let's get you suited up." I feel the warmth of his hand on my arm, and it begins flooding through me again. We walk like that for a bit, not talking, just listening to Anna chatter on. I can feel a tingle way deep inside me as we walk, which only gets more intense when he smiles at me.

"Okay. Most of the stuff you already know, but there's a couple of things that are specific to fur characters." Luke helps zip up the back of my costume. I can already feel myself begin to sweat, even though we're still inside in the air-conditioning. "First, your center of gravity is way higher in the costume; so if a little kid comes barreling at your knees, bend forward to keep from falling on your tail."

"Literally," I say, turning and twitching my hips to make my fur tail bounce. I see Luke's cheeks get pink, which makes me blush. He clears his throat.

"Second, you need to remember that you have no peripheral vision once you get the head on, so we'll need to help each other maneuver in the crowds. That's why you rarely see fur characters by themselves."

"Except Foulfellow," I say.

"That's only because he has these mirrors sewn into the wristbands of his coat."

"And you can't do that, because you're naked." I watch him blush even deeper.

"Finally," he says, and his voice is a little softer, "if you get into trouble, like someone has you cornered or you just need a break, do this." He points to his nose.

"That's the signal?"

"Do you have a better one?" Luke asks, lifting up Chip's head. I shake my head, then hold still so he can mount the fur head, clipping it to little straps along the neckline of the costume.

"You don't think anyone will know, do you?"

"That you're not Cassie?" he says. I bend my head so that I can see out of the eyeholes. "No one will know. I mean, *I'd* know."

"I'd hope so," I say, and my voice sounds close and loud inside the head. "She is your girlfriend."

"That's not what I mean," Luke says, clipping his head in place and walking over, so that our noses are almost touching. "I don't mean I would know it wasn't Cassie in there. I mean, I'd know it was you." I'm glad he can't see my face inside the head because if he did, he'd see my cheeks turn deep red.

"You were amazing," Luke says, punching the code into the panel beside the locked door.

"Nah," I say, stepping inside as he holds the door open for me. We walk forward, past a cart full of character juice cups and empty popcorn boxes. "Can we take these off?" I ask, pointing to my nose.

"Sure, this tunnel spits us out right behind the front staging area." He helps me free my head from my shoulders and lifts it off.

"I must look like a drowned rat," I say, using my paw to push my hair away from my forehead. Luke puts my head on the floor and unbuckles his own head.

"Drowned rodent," he says, laughing.

I lift my head and flip it over, holding it by its inside lip. We start walking along the corridor, passing different tunnels that can take you to anywhere in the park. "Luke, can I ask you something?"

"Chipmunk to chipmunk?"

I smile over at him, and he nods. "What makes you happy?" He's quiet for a few moments, and we walk, listening to the soft pat of our feet on the concrete floor.

"That's a tough one," he says. "I guess there are easy answers like, I don't know, when my car is all washed and waxed, or thunderstorms, or a good cup of coffee. But then there are the more complicated ones."

"Like what?"

"Love, family . . . the usual." We walk for a few moments. "Now, why did that make you quiet?"

"Just thinking," I say, shifting my head to my other hand.

"Can I ask you something?"

"Chipmunk to chipmunk?"

He nods, then stops walking and faces me. I stop, too, and lean back against the wall of the tunnel. "Why are you so sad?" I look at my fur feet and try to come up with a smart-ass answer, but I can't. I can feel the tears in my eyes, and suddenly, they're spilling down the front of me, making drops on the fur. "Ella, I'm sorry," he says, reaching out and touching my arm. "I didn't mean to make you cry."

"It's okay," I say, and take a deep breath. "Do you really want to know?" I ask, looking up at him. He nods, and I take another breath and tell him. Tell him everything.

Luke

For a while there, it seemed like everybody was totally down with the idea for Dalebration. Some people passed around a list of their un-favorite party foods (Funyuns, honey mustard potato chips, bacon-flavored pretzels), and went searching out the off-brand sodas (Mountain Juice, Dr. Wham), and the music was going to be a bunch of one-hit wonders, and everyone was going through the lost-and-found box to pick out some hand-me-downs to wear. Then everything started going to crap. First off, most of the Lesser Characters, as we started calling them, didn't like thinking of themselves that way, and a few were even insulted. Is it my fault nobody ever heard of Jim Hawkins or Perla the Mouse? That no one ever wants their autograph or pictures? They spend their days walking around the park like homeless people, followed by voices saying over and over, "Daddy, who's that?" "I don't know, sweetie." You grow bitter over time, I guess. Then, when it was determined that we had a shortage of women signed on, Robin Hood and the Merry Men dropped out, and of course, the Army Men do whatever the Merry Men do (I sometimes imagine the Army Men's mothers saying, "If those Merry Men jumped off a cliff . . ."), and now even Amy doesn't want to go, because Jesse isn't going, and that's that.

"Well, listen," Mark says, "who said you can't have a party with just four people?"

"I don't know," I say. "Abraham Lincoln?"

It's the end of dinner in the cafeteria, just me and Cassie and Mark and Ella. The food tonight was the worst ever: hot dogs with packets of ketchup, and instant lemonade. This starts a brand-new round of rumors that they are about to settle the strike, that they aren't buying any new food for us. The picketers have been missing for two days now, so who knows.

"No, no," Mark says, missing my joke, "I mean that we can still *have* the party."

"That's okay," I say. "I'll drop the idea. No prophet is accepted in his own country."

Ella laughs. "So it was a mystical vision, your plans for Dalebration?"

Cassie frowns. "Luke, what are you talking about? If they don't want to party, screw them, you know?"

I nod, but I'm looking at Ella, smiling. "The whole thing came to me in a dream."

"No, it came to you during a banana-split-related social gathering, remember?"

"Yeah, but who says I wasn't dreaming?"

Cassie slides in closer to me, her hand on my thigh. "I have a cool idea," she says. "Forget the party. The four of us will just go out, get a *real* dinner for a change. A double date."

"Yeah," Mark says, "and maybe we can combine contest lists, since, you know, it's really for all of us in the end. The prizes, I mean."

"Right," I tell him. "We'll tell you about all *three* things that we've found." He laughs, and I glance at Ella, whose face looks like I imagine my own to look. A little sick to her stomach.

"Then it's settled, okay?" Cassie says, an edge in her voice. "Tomorrow night?"

I remember once in Mr. Forrester's office, his calendar said "Keep Your Friends Close and Your Enemies Closer," and I imagine that's what Cassie is doing right now. Get Ella on her own turf, make a show of holding my hand, kissing me.

She'd been like this since two days before, when she and Mark were coming back from list hunting and Ella and I were walking out of the tunnel in the Chip and Dale costumes, carrying our heads. Ella was still crying while I rubbed her shoulder.

"Well, look who's here," Cassie said, her smile frozen in place. "So . . . what's all this?"

"This is you not showing up for work," I said.

"And she was all broken up about it?" she said, waving her clipboard at Ella.

"Cassie, lay off," I said. "She's upset."

"Ella, what's wrong?" Mark said. "Why are you wearing *that*?"

"Aww, sweetheart, I'm really sorry," Cassie said, putting her hand on Ella's fur arm. "I didn't know, and I'm being insensitive. Why don't we go talk about it, just us girls?" More and more it was like some layer had been peeled away from Cassie, so I could see what was really there. And what was really there was mostly fake. Sometimes I think that layer was just my own naïveté, wanting to believe that people are what they seem to be. And what Cassie seemed to be was how she was being now, with Ella. But that wasn't real, either, just something put on for the benefit of everyone else, just another costume she wore.

"I'm fine, really," Ella said. "It's just the heat and all. I'm fine."

"Ella, why are you *wearing* that?" Mark said, like maybe a change in emphasis would make the question work better. The costume seemed to be his only worry. For him, probably a big enough worry to make his head explode—if Cinderella could turn into Chip, what next? Ariel turning into Minnie Mouse? Belle turning into Dopey? Maybe Snow White would turn into Daffy Duck, *who wasn't even a Disney character*. Really, it would be a lot like the Apocalypse.

"Try to figure it out, Mark," Ella had said before walking off.

Now Ella glances at me across the cafeteria table and shakes her head just slightly so that only I can see it.

"You know," Cassie says, leaning harder into me, "there are like a ton of really good restaurants here. So, maybe you two pick a time, and Luke and I will pick a place. How does that sound?"

"Well, you know," I say, "I bet you don't want to miss a whole night of working on your list, do you?"

I'm looking at Mark as I say it, and if the Jedi mind trick worked, even a little bit, right now he would be saying, *I don't want to miss a whole night*. Instead, he just looks at Cassie, who smiles and says, "Oh, everyone needs a little rest," and Mark nods and agrees, yes, they do need a rest. Maybe the mind trick *does* work. Ella doesn't say anything but just keeps looking at me or glancing down at Cassie's hand on my arm, until I want to just pull it away. Instead, I just try finding a few more outs, and of course, Cassie bats them all down. "It will be the most fun ever, I swear," she says, and by now she has worn us all down, worn all the excuses out, and so the plans are made.

Late that night I walk out behind the castle, in the shadows of the leaves. I'm looking for Ella, but our bench is empty. I sit there, anyway, and reach up to pull a leaf from the tree, and then tear off bits of leaf to throw at my sneakers. It beats sleeping, which is getting harder to come by every night. All I've been able to do for the past two days is think about Ella, about everything she told me. I don't even know how to think about something huge like that, like it's all the hurt someone usually has over a whole lifetime wadded up into one ball and dropped from a height. And that's how I picture it, like maybe it doesn't totally kill you, but it breaks both your legs, and they never heal right, and for the rest of your life you walk with a limp. If Ben died, it *would* kill me, no broken legs. I know that, and so I think about how strong she must be inside, how she can get up in the morning, and it's not like she's off to work filing papers in some back office. No, she's out there every day, looking beautiful, smiling for everyone. She is nice to the little kids—*really* nice, not the kind of nice that they teach us in the character seminars, not fake nice, not scripted nice.

Not Cassie nice.

And part of me felt stupid, too, when she told me. I mean, I did everything I was supposed to do, not because I was supposed to, but because it was just what you do—she was talking and I listened, really listened, not just to her words, but to the way she took small breaths between words; listened to the rustle of her hair against her fur costume as she tipped her head back when the tears came, listened to the slight quaver in her voice and to how unfamiliar the words sounded coming from her, like she had never really said them to anyone before. That's how you listen. And then she cried, but not as much as you'd think. Maybe there had been so much of that already, or maybe after a time it just seemed like not enough. But I held her as well as I could with both of us in costume, and for about five minutes I felt like an idiot because I've been freaked out about what? Taking a good job? That's my tragedy? "I had tuberculosis as a child." "Oh yeah? Well, I had to share a corner office."

But that seems wrong, too, finally. I mean, both of us are trapped inside something, like mirror images of ourselves and each other. She's trapped inside her loss, inside everything that's missing from her life, trying to breathe in a vacuum. And me? The opposite—I'm trapped inside everything that's given to me, handed to me, placed on top of me, as I try to breathe under a thick pile of expectation. Her future had been dismantled under her, and mine was constructed over me. And neither of us has a way of escaping. Unless maybe we do—I think the most hopeful moment of my life was when we were in the Chip and Dale costumes, holding hands while we danced in a circle, and I could hear her laughing a little bit inside there, could barely see her through the mesh, and I laughed just because she was, just because we were so dumb and she didn't know the routine and we were just winging it, winging the whole thing, and I kept thinking, *We're in here . . . hidden, smaller than the thing around us, but still inside here.* If only your life were a costume, and you could just take it off when you wanted to, leave it hanging on a hook, and walk away.

I take another long look down the quiet walk that leads toward the castle, hoping I will see her, that she will know I'm out here and come find me. I have so much to tell her. Everything, really. But there are only a few browned palm boughs, blowing around in the wind, and as much as I want her to be, she's not there.

The next day, before I'm even out of bed, my mother calls. For a little while we talk about the weather and how hot it is and how Dad is away on some project and how Ben is learning to play golf, taking lessons at the club every evening.

"Golf is a wise business move," she says, though I can tell she's just quoting Ben.

"I thought it was a game played with sticks and balls," I say.

"Well, it's that, too, silly. But Ben says it will help him woo clients."

I nod at the phone. "Did he actually say 'woo'?"

"Yes, I believe. Why?"

"Tell him that's gay. That I said so."

She tries not to laugh. "I will tell him no such thing."

"How is Dad with the headaches?" Our phone is this old-school black thing mounted to the wall of the dorm, and every time I talk on it, I end up tangling the curly cord around my wrist.

"Oh," she says, "his life is a headache, I guess. But he's fine. He just works too hard."

"Why?"

"That's a silly question, Luke. You work hard, too, don't you? I know you do. And we're all proud of you."

"I do. If there is some chipmunkin' that needs doing, I am *on* the job." I spin my wrist around trying to free it from the twists of cord.

"We all want to know when you'll be home," she says. "We have so much planned for you."

I feel my stomach knot up. *So much planned for me,* I think. *Like maybe the next fifty years.* "I don't know," I tell her. There is a brief silence, the conversation shutting down; then without really knowing what I want to say, I ask her, "Mom, what happened?"

"What happened when, honey?" I can see her face when she says it, the way she will look at someone so quizzically, but with all this patience, too, like she wants to know something and you have all the time in the world to tell her.

"I mean . . ." I stall for a second. "I meant, What will happen the rest of the day? Your day."

"Oh, well." She sighs. "The usual, I guess. I am getting my hair cut at one. And then I'm meeting with Sandy to talk about the rummage sale at the church. And I need to take the Honda in for an oil change. Big excitement, huh?"

"Could be worse. I mean, you have no major disasters planned, huh?"

She laughs and says maybe tomorrow, and I have that urge to ask her again, What happened? Instead, I tell her I love her, untangle the phone from my wrist, and hang up.

We head to Shula's because Cassie says it's the best place in the whole resort. Robin Hood hooks me up with a jacket and a white shirt, and I wear my boots and good jeans, so it's not half-bad. When Cassie shows up at the dorm to walk over with me, she's wearing this little brown, pin-striped skirt, pretty much up to her ass, and these tall heels, her legs tanned and perfect, and a tight pink sweater, her hair all blow-dried and loose. Robin Hood hands her the knife he's using to make a peanut butter sandwich. "Kill me now," he says, and she laughs like it's the best joke she's ever heard. All throughout the common room the Merry Men and Army Men are whistling and screeching, and Jesse walks by and just solemnly pats my shoulder and tells me that it nearly makes him want to weep. And she does look amazing in a way—I mean, I'm not immune, but I guess I end up feeling like an accessory as we walk along. Or maybe more like a prop, built with an arm that's designed to be held in her grip. Plus I'm not a big fan of makeup, and she has on enough to kill someone.

"This place is superfantastic," Mark says as we meet them in the lobby, and right away I cut my eyes at Ella, and she tries not to smile. She looks beautiful—just this pretty flowered dress, her shoulders pale and freckled, her dark hair in loose waves, tiny diamond studs in her ears. Simple, sweet, perfect. Mark wears a Mickey tie and a shirt with Donald and Daisy cuff links, and he has his hair combed exactly the way it is when he plays Prince Charming.

"You look so cute all dressed up," Cassie tells Ella, and Ella just smiles and tells Cassie she looks like a million bucks. Cassie reaches out and adjusts Mark's tie. "Boys are so messy sometimes," she says, and winks at Ella. Mark starts in telling us about the history of the building while the hostess takes us to a table, and by the time we sit, he has moved on to facts about Bay Lake, which is just outside the big window at the far end of the restaurant.

"You want to hear something weird?" he says. "If you look at old satellite maps of Orlando, back before the park was built, Bay Lake was shaped like Mickey. It's not anymore because they filled in part of one ear when they built the park, but it was then. Like a perfect Mickey."

"Mark, you just know so much, it's scary sometimes," Cassie says. Under the table she digs her fingernails into my thigh. She has told me ten times before that if she has to listen to another Disney fun-fact, she is going to commit suicide with a pair of mouse ears. I kind of know what she means, but at the same time some of the stuff he digs up actually is interesting. I mean, if I didn't have to watch him touching Ella all the time, I could probably even like the guy.

"So, you've looked at old satellite maps of Orlando?" Ella asks him.

He shrugs. "Just the one time. But I just think it's weird

that a Mickey lake was here like a thousand years ago. Makes you think some things really are meant to be, you know?"

I glance at Ella just as she glances at me, and for that moment my heart stops. She blushes and pokes at her salad plate with her fork.

"Are you okay, Ella?" Cassie says.

"I'm fine. I'm glad you picked this place," she says. "It's really nice."

"Well, *we* picked it," she says, grabbing my arm. I feel my face heat up and want to remind her that I never heard of this place before tonight, but I don't. I mean, why bother? Then again, some part of me does want to bother, with all of it—wants to jerk my arm away and take Ella out of there and keep walking; to call my dad and Ben and tell them I won't be working for them, not next year, maybe not ever; to find some place where Ella feels there is ground under her feet, at least enough to start moving forward again instead of always looking back. Then I think something like that might work in a movie, but I'm just here on a double date with some-one I really don't even like very much, and her hand is on my leg and I am buttering a roll and later we will kiss. And tomorrow I will have to show up for work, Cassie will still be my girlfriend, Ella will still be with Mark and think of me as only her pal, and somehow the sameness of one moment will keep turning into the sameness of the next. And I never know how to make it stop.

Mark isn't quite finished, and for once I'm grateful. The

whole dinner I keep trying not to sneak looks at Ella, but I can't help myself, and then Cassie notices and climbs a little farther into my lap, and Ella just looks sad. I don't know which is worse. Right now, Mark is a welcome distraction. He tells us about all the Hidden Mickeys in the park, including one made from stalagmites on the Pirates of the Caribbean ride, or the watermark on every receipt printed in the park. He has memorized about two hundred, he tells us, though there are hundreds more.

"And get this," he says, slicing the last of his prime rib, "Disney is actually a *town*, separate from Orlando. I just found this out yesterday. Those security guards are real cops. I mean, there are cast members who act as the city council, and another cast member who serves as mayor."

"Is it you?" I say, and the others laugh, including Mark.

"You see what this means?" he says. "It really is a *real* place. And the cool part, so that they can actually establish a government, someone has to live here, in the park. I mean, people have their regular houses here, do their laundry, put their kids on the bus. How cool is that?"

Ella looks at me. "Well, that explains Bernard," she says.

"I guess," I tell her. "He's just a tool of corporate government. He had that look about him."

She laughs. "Actually, maybe *he's* the mayor."

"Who took my job?" Mark says, and laughs.

"What are you talking about?" Cassie says suddenly. "Who is Bernard?" Her face is flushed.

"That phantom guy. I told you about all of that. J. Worthington Foulfellow? We went to his place for a visit." I finish my meal but only vaguely remember eating it.

She turns to Ella. "And you went? I didn't know about that. Luke just said some of the guys went."

"I said some *people* went," I tell her. "Next time I'll give you a full report, okay?"

"Well, it's not that," she says, turning her full smile back on. "It's just that I might like to get invited next time. And I would think Ella would be scared of something like that. I mean, he sounds creepy, you know?"

"Interesting he wants to be that character," Mark says. "He could move up if he wanted."

"I wasn't scared, and he wasn't creepy," Ella says, looking at Cassie. "I liked him quite a bit."

"And I like that about you," Cassie says, using her best honey-coated voice. "Nothing gets to you. Even when I see you walking around here all sad, you bounce right back. I mean, you are just unapproachable somehow, let nothing in. I so much admire that. Me? I'm too emotional."

Ella just looks at her a full five seconds. And then she starts laughing. Trying to hold it in, hand to her mouth, but she is laughing, and I start laughing a little bit just because she is, and there are tears forming in her eyes. Mark raises his hand and asks the waiter for the check.

"What did I say that's so funny?" Cassie says.

Ella drinks her water, dabs her eyes with her napkin. "You invented a new part of speech," she says. "The complimentary insult. I call it the *complisult*. Like it?"

"Hey, Ella," I say. "I have never seen hair quite like that."

"*That's* what I'm talking about," she says. "And Luke, you know, knowing you has taught me that determination is more important than brains."

"I didn't mean—" Cassie starts to say.

"Yes, you did," Ella says, "but really, it's okay. I promise. Mark, let's hear yours."

He thinks for a minute, blushing. "I'm sure," he finally says, "that I will never eat another meal like this one."

"Man, good one," Ella says.

"And hey, Mark?" I say. "It's great the way you play Prince Charming so he appeals to people of all sexual orientations."

Mark lets that one sink in before deciding it's okay to laugh. Ella dabs at her eyes a little bit. "You know," Mark says, "I love your jacket. Is that real polyester?"

By now Ella can't stop laughing, and some of the people at other tables are starting to look over at us. Cassie smiles, but the smile looks like it was forged from ice and piano wire.

"Well," she says, "you guys are crazy. How about if we get out of here?"

And so we do, walking out into the warm Florida night, with the breeze stirring paper cups and discarded napkins along the walk. I'm ready to just bail on this, cut our losses, but I guess Cassie isn't done. It's like she won't be done until she wins, though I'm not sure what it is she's trying to win. All I know is, I'm tired.

"I know," she says, "let's head over to downtown and shop, just look in the windows or something. Maybe Ella and I will model something for you boys, if you're lucky." She winks at Mark and he blushes, then she squeezes my arm, pulling it against her breast, and part of me just wants to tell her to stop, to quit trying so hard. But I'm beginning to think she never will, not in her whole life.

We walk through the candy stores and Ella and I get the big box of Junior Mints while Mark goes for the Kit Kat, and Cassie says that chocolate goes straight to her hips.

"It really hardly shows on you," she says to Ella.

Ella nods. "All right," she says. "Good one, Cass."

Cassie narrows her eyes for a moment before flipping her hair and turning away.

From there we head through the Cirque du Soleil store, looking at the paintings, and then to the Mickey's Mart— Everything Ten Dollars and Under store, which is Disney's jacked-up version of a dollar store and has a little bit of everything.

"This place is crap," Cassie says. "Let's go to the World of Disney Store."

"We pretty much *are* the Disney Store," I tell her. "I like this place."

"I do, too," Ella says. Cassie starts muttering, actually muttering to herself, under her breath, like someone in a movie. I ought to feel bad, but why? I'm having too much fun. Even Mark seems pretty cool.

"We should get a souvenir," he says. "I mean, to remember tonight."

"Yes, Mark. We will want to remember tonight forever." I look at Ella while Cassie sulks, and she smiles at me, winks. I love that moment so much, all the sadness gone from her, that I think I already have my souvenir. We look around for a bit and can't really decide.

"Because this stuff is crap," Cassie says. "Tourist crap." She sits in a little kid's Mickey chair.

"Man," I say, "crappy souvenirs in a theme park. Frankly, I'm shocked."

"I just can't decide," Ella says.

"I have an idea," I say. I call over one of the assistant managers, this girl who's maybe five years older than we are. She's funny looking, in a good way, with about a billion freckles and this kinky reddish hair and tiny blue frames for her glasses. Her name tag says MANDY. She's wearing a smiley-face button and a Mickey button, and she has drawn mustaches on both with a Sharpie.

"Pool your money," I tell the others. "Cough it up."

"Why?" Cassie says.

"That's a secret," I say.

"Then you aren't getting my money."

I nod and turn to Mark, who says he only brought a credit

card, and then Ella, who gives me ten bucks. I put in ten of my own and hand it to Mandy.

"Okay, Mandy," I tell her. "We are buying a surprise gift. Can you help us?"

She shrugs. "Sure thang," she says. "Who is the surprise for?"

"For us," I tell her. "Take the money, take a good look at us, and buy something that you know, you *know*, we will like. Buy it, box it up, and don't let us see it, okay?"

She smiles, then spends a long time sizing us up, looking us over before nodding and heading off.

"That's pretty cool," Mark says. "Buy yourself a surprise gift."

"Pretty stupid, you mean, right?" Cassie says, still sitting in the chair. She looks tired, too, both of us tired. "She's going to buy you a five-buck gift, box it up, and pocket the rest."

"No," I say, looking not at her but at Ella, who is looking right back at me. "She's going to give us exactly what we want."

Ella

"Where do you want to go?" Luke keeps watching me with this half grin on his face.

I pull my feet up on the bench. "To the moon?"

"Okay, ding-dong. Somewhere in the park."

"Ding-dong? We're at the name-calling phase of our relationship?"

"Ella, we need to focus here." Luke slides his hands into the pockets of his jeans and rocks on the balls of his feet. The same grin. The same light that keeps flickering across his eyes. "Where in the *park* do you want to go?"

"Anywhere?" I tilt my head and look up at the handful of stars that can shine through the light of the park.

"Anywhere."

"I want to see the inside of the castle." I smile back at

him, knowing it's an impossible task. No one goes inside the castle. Not even the security guards.

"Done," Luke says, raising his eyebrow. I hear a jingle in his pocket. "Close your eyes. I want to show you something." I close my eyes and wait. I hear the jingle again, louder as he pulls his hand free of his pocket. "Okay," he says. "Open them."

"You want to show me your keys?" I look at the ring of maybe fifty keys dangling from his hand. "It does take a real man to pull off a Tinker Bell key chain."

"Okay, ding-dong. These are not my keys."

"Again with the ding-dong."

Luke fishes in his pocket again and pulls out a folded piece of paper. "These are Bernard's keys. And this," he says, passing me the paper, "is a list that tells you what key we need to go anywhere in the park."

"Where did he get all those?" I ask, reaching out to brush my fingers against the keys hanging lowest on the chain.

"He just told me that thirty years on the force has its benefits."

"The Force. That must have resonated with you, young Jedi."

Luke sighs and rolls his eyes. "You're never going to stop, are you?"

"Of course," I say, unfolding the paper and scanning down the list. I look back up at Luke and smile. "Like maybe when we're seventy."

"No you won't," he says. "We'll be sitting out on the front porch on our rockers, half deaf, complaining about our rheumatism, and you'll still be cracking *Star Wars* jokes."

I lower my voice as low as it can go and breathe slowly and heavily. "I find your lack of faith disturbing." I start laughing before I can even finish.

"How do you *know* all this stuff?" Luke asks, squinting at me. "I mean, I get the obvious ones, but that's pretty obscure Darth Vader."

"Ash was a real *Star Wars* freak." It's the second time in a long time that I've said his name out loud. Both times to Luke. And when I'm talking to him, it feels okay. It feels just right, like this is exactly where I'm supposed to be. Doing exactly what I'm supposed to be doing. "How about you? You must know tons of stuff."

"Not me," he says, jangling the keys. "I think on a much higher plane than that. I spend my time asking life's bigger questions."

"Like, who ate the last brownie?"

"That was *one* time." He smiles at me and reaches for my free hand. "Come on, Princess. We have a castle to check out." We walk in silence for a few minutes, his fingers woven into mine. I'm almost afraid to breathe. Afraid to break the bubble around us. Afraid if I do, he'll let go of my hand. Luke looks over at me and smiles. "Wonderful girl. Either I'm going to kill her or I'm beginning to like her." This time we both laugh, and underneath it all I can feel his fingers tighten around mine, trapping each one with his. He's inside the bubble, too, and both of us are holding our breath.

It was weird ending the date, if you could even call it that. It was more like three friends going out to eat and shopping, and taking along their very beautiful and very angry pit bull. Even before we could all get through the doorway into the dorm, Cassie had said good night and was climbing the stairs to the second floor.

"I think that went well," Mark said, smiling at us.

"Sarcasm?" Luke said, running his fingers through his hair. "This is a weird night."

"So are you going to look in the box?" Mark asked, pointing to the cardboard shoe box tucked under Luke's arm.

"Should we?" Luke asked. He looked at me, and I shook my head.

"Let's wait until tomorrow. Get a little space between tonight and the surprise." What I didn't say is that I wanted to open it when it was just Luke and me.

"Good idea," Luke said, lifting the box up to his ear and shaking it slightly.

"No fair peeking." I pushed his shoulder, then noticed Mark looking at us, watching us; but when he saw me looking at him, he just smiled.

"You going up?" I asked Mark. He nodded at me and turned toward the stairs.

"I'm going to stay up for a while," Luke said, turning

toward the TV room. He looked back at me once before disappearing around the corner.

"Hey," I said, catching up with Mark on the stairs. "Thank you. It was fun." I reached out and briefly touched the collar of his shirt, sliding the soft fabric through my fingers.

"It was, wasn't it?" he asked, putting his hand over mine. "Ella, it's okay, you know." He squeezed my hand with his.

"What is?" I tilted my head at him, watching. He leaned back against the wall and smiled at me.

"You aren't going to make this easy on me, are you?" I shifted a bit and leaned against the wall straight across from him and looked down at my feet. "Ella, anyone can see it. I mean, *everyone* can see it."

"Luke . . ." I said, my voice barely above a whisper. We stayed like that for a few moments, listening to the noises spilling down on us from the floors above. A series of thuds followed by a door slamming, and then footsteps coming down the stairs.

"You two should be together," Mark said softly. The footsteps stopped a couple of stairs up from where I was standing. Around the corner and out of my sight. "Hey," Mark said to the person standing there.

"Am I interrupting anything?" Robin Hood asked, jumping down the remaining steps and landing with a thud next to where Mark was standing.

"Just talking," I said, still staring at my feet.

"You okay, Princess?" Robin Hood asked. I just nodded without looking up at him.

"I was just telling her that sometimes the prince and princess don't live happily ever after. At least not together," Mark said. I looked up at him, but he was still smiling.

"You're dumping her?" Robin Hood asked.

"I'm right here," I said.

"Not exactly," Mark said, shifting so that he was looking more at Robin Hood than at me.

"She's dumping you? Man, bitches. You can't live with them—"

"I'm still right here," I said. "No one is dumping anyone."

"I was just telling her that maybe she needs to rethink her fairy tale," Mark said.

"Maybe get a little chipmunk action," Robin Hood said. He laughed, and Mark and I looked up at him. "What?" Robin Hood said. "You know it's true. I just gave your roommate her laundry payment. Looks like Prince Charming beat me to it with you."

"How's that?" I asked. He just rolled his eyes at me and jabbed Mark in the shoulder.

"Come on, Prince. What do you say to a couple beers to chase away the heartache?"

"Sure," Mark said. "Just give me a minute."

Robin Hood pushed past us and down the stairs. We listened as the heavy sounds of his footsteps grew fainter. Then his voice from downstairs: "Luke, my man. We were just talking about you."

Mark shook his head and smiled at me.

"It really is okay, Ella." He touched my cheek with the tips of his fingers. "The thing about fairy tales is, they're only as real as you make them." He smiled again, shrugged. "I think I will have a beer. Maybe two."

"Wow," I said as he stepped past me and started making his way down to where I could still hear Robin Hood talking to Luke. "It really *is* a weird night."

"The weirdest," Mark said. I kept standing there until I could hear his voice along with the other two, then I headed up to my room.

"We'll have to be pretty quiet," Luke says, squeezing my fingers before releasing my hand. "When I was here earlier, I dropped the keys, and it sounded like the whole castle exploded. Something about the acoustics in here." He's right. Even whispering several feet away from me, Luke sounds like he's talking normally, maybe even loudly, right in my ear.

"Wait, what do you mean, when you were here earlier?"

"I had something to drop off," he says, climbing the stairs to the balcony, but instead of taking a right out to where I usually greet my wedding guests, he veers left and climbs another short flight of stairs to a door marked PRIVATE. I stand on the step just below him and place my hand on the small of his back. He looks over his shoulder briefly, smiling at me and then back at the ring of keys in his hand. "Here it is," he says, freeing a key with the number 17 printed on it in black marker. He presses the key into the lock, turning it once to the right. "It sticks a bit," he says, pulling the handle toward himself.

"How do you know?"

"I told you, I was here earlier. I didn't want to get here and have the key not work."

"How did you know I'd pick the castle?" Luke pushes down again on the handle, and the door pops free from its jamb with a sharp snap, which echoes down the stairs.

"*Shhh*," I say, pressing my face into the center of his back to keep from laughing.

"*Shhh*, yourself," he says. "Come on. I didn't go all the way in before. I didn't want to see it without you."

"How will we be able to see anything?" I ask, stepping up and through the doorway after him.

"You'll find I'm full of surprises." Luke reaches down and feels around on the floor before standing. "Here, you hold this," he says, handing me our surprise box. "Voilà." Suddenly, the whole area we are standing in is bathed in a pale pink light. I look at the flashlight in his hand.

"Disney Princess. Nice touch."

"I was going to go with the Cruella De Vil one, but it was a red light. Somehow that didn't really seem like the atmosphere I was going for."

"Luke?" I shift the box into one hand and put my other

on his arm. "In case I forget to tell you later, I had a great time tonight."

"Me, too," he says, smiling. "You want to go in?"

"Do chipmunks dance?"

He laughs softly and takes my hand again, leading me into the darkness.

This whole night with Luke feels like one of those pictures that they have at the mall, the ones on the cart across from the pretzel place or Orange Julius or in front of Lids or Hot Topic. They're made up of repeating squares or interlocking circles or quadrafoils turned on end. They look like bad cubist paintings. Too much symmetry, not enough dissonance. Sometimes there's a card beside them, telling you what you're supposed to be looking for. Telling you to try and see two people kissing or a dolphin in the ocean or the image of Elvis—the young one, not the fried peanut butter and banana sandwich one. More often than not, there isn't a sign. You just have to stand there and look, trying to see past the patterns to the picture hidden within them, You can't take your eyes off it. You let your focus soften. Let yourself fall into it. If you blink or if you look away for even a second, you have to start all over again, resetting yourself. Sometimes you can look and look and not see anything. You hear people around you. "Do you see it? Right *there*. There's the nose. There's the guitar. Do you see it?" And you think about giving up. You think that no matter how long you keep looking, nothing will happen. That all the people around you are just telling everyone they can see it so they won't look stupid. But then you *do* see it. And once you see it, you can't stop seeing it. Now, instead of seeing the blue squares marching off into infinity, replicating themselves like microscopic organisms, you see the lion's face or Lincoln or the unicorn. And once you see it, you turn to the strangers around you. "Do you see it?" you ask. Because once you see it, you want everyone to know. You want everyone else to see it, too.

"Do you believe in ghosts?" I ask, following Luke through the archway and into the main room. I bump against something hard with my hip.

"Yes," Luke says, stopping and turning to look at me.

"Okay, not really the answer I was hoping for," I say, smiling at him. His face is glowing pink from the Princess flashlight.

"Well, I don't believe in sheet-over-the-head, rattling-chains, creaking-stairs-in-the-middle-of-the-night ghosts." Luke turns and looks toward one of the windows at the far side of the room. One of the thin ones you can see from the outside. Diamonds of metal crisscross the glass, making it look quilted. "It's more subtle. It's like all of us are haunted all the time, but we usually never know it." Luke walks over to a large shape near the wall that looks in the darkness like a snowman with a huge hat on his head. "I don't think they'll be able to see this with the spotlights on the castle." He clicks something near the top of the snowman, just under the hat, and the lamp lights up.

"Wow. It's like Retroland," I say, looking around the room. "This stuff is amazing." I run my palm over the top of the couch, feeling its nubby texture beneath my hand. An orange and turquoise light that resembles an exotic tropical flower towers over a leather chair in the corner. Most of the side wall is taken up by a clock with huge metal rays shooting off in every direction. Steel and wood and molded plastic share space with hooked rugs and silk pillows. "It's like *The Brady Bunch* meets *The Jetsons*," I say, touching a vase that seems made up entirely of plastic bubbles in shades of orange and green.

"Bernard told me some of the Disney elite built this so they could stay here." I walk around the end of the couch and toward the windows looking out on Main Street. "This place looks like a really tasteful Goodwill," he says. I smile over at Luke, who's looking at a chess set, only three pieces out of their opening positions.

"Want to see what's in the box?" I ask, pointing to the taped shoe box I set down on the couch.

"Well, yeah." Luke says, grinning at me. He picks up the box and walks toward me. "Want to do the honors?" he asks.

"No, you."

He runs his thumb along the tape line, pulling the top free. "Ready?" he asks. I nod and watch as he flips the top off the shoe box, reaches into the folded tissue paper, and extracts a bundle. "Now you," he says, handing it to me. I peel back the layers of paper, revealing a snow globe. One of the windup ones that makes the figures dance through the snow. "Wind it up," he says. The opening chimes of "When You Wish Upon a Star" tinkle out as a tiny Cinderella and Prince Charming begin their slow waltz around the castle.

"Look at the front," I say, turning it to face him.

"Dreams can come true," he reads. He stops smiling and turns to look out the other window facing Main Street.

"Tell me more about your ghosts," I say, watching him for a moment before turning to look back out the window. The one right over the crest with Walt's name in it. "Tell me what you meant about our lives being haunted."

"I don't know, Ella. It's not like I have this all figured out."

"I think you do. I think you have a lot more figured out than you let on," I say, still looking out the window. From this angle I can see the wire Tinker Bell flies on stretching toward Tomorrowland.

"I think it isn't so much that we are haunted by something on the outside," he says. "It's more like we make our own ghosts out of our hopes and disappointments, and then dress them up with the wishes that other people have for us."

"Like costumes," I say, turning to look at him.

"Exactly. It's like we have these hopes for ourselves. These fairy tales for our lives. We think we know how to live happily ever after, but we let other people take over and put shackles on our dreams, so that even if we wanted them to, they can hardly move."

I nod and look down at my feet. Luke walks over to where I'm standing and puts his fingertips under my chin, lifting my face until I'm looking at him. "Here's the secret I've figured out. You ready?" I nod again, feeling my chest tightening as I try not to breathe. "The trick is, we have the keys. Whenever we want to, we can unlock the chains."

"Do you really think that's true?" I ask. He is standing close enough for me to see the shimmery flecks of gold in his eyes.

"Ella, you asked me a question a long time ago, and I didn't really know how to answer it." He keeps looking at me while he's talking. Really looking at me, like he can see way inside me. "You asked me if I believed in magic. Do you remember?"

"Do you?" I whisper.

"I wasn't sure before tonight. I wasn't sure yesterday. But with you here and even this," he says, pointing to the snow globe resting on the windowsill. He looks back at me and traces my jawline with his fingers, so lightly that they're just a whisper against my skin. "Only magic could explain all of this," he says, leaning forward. I close my eyes as I feel his breath against my lips. "Ella?" he whispers. I open my eyes again to see him smiling.

"Yes?"

"Kiss me you will," he whispers. And then we do.

· · ·

I keep thinking the sky is going to start turning pink at any minute. The sun is going to come up, but it doesn't. We have to walk back across the park to the dorm. It takes a long time because we have to duck behind trees and into doorways as morning maintenance people filter through the park, getting everything ready. "Listen," Luke says, tugging at my hand when we draw even with the trees bordering the dorm courtyard. I stop and face him. "I have some things to take care of when I wake up."

"Things . . ." I say, smiling.

"Well, I have to return the keys to Bernard and then . . . well, there's Cassie."

"There is Cassie," I say, tilting my head and watching his face.

"Hey," he says, sliding his hand around my waist and pulling me to him. "Who did I just spend the last four hours kissing?"

"Anyone I know?"

He bends down and kisses me again, and again I feel it all the way through me, so that instead of just kissing my mouth, it feels like he's kissing all of my cells at the same time. And again when he stops, it feels like I've been spinning around and around in the teacups with my eyes closed because I have to hold on to him to keep from falling over.

"So, listen," he says. "I'll meet you. Breakfast. Okay?" I just nod and lean against him. "And don't be late," he tells me. "No sleeping in. I almost missed out on you completely. I don't want to miss another minute."

"No," I say. "Neither do I."

Luke

My head is so blurry with no sleep that a shower doesn't even help much. When Robin Hood has had another long, bad night, he wakes himself up by dunking three tea bags into a cup of black coffee and gulping it down. But I'm not hungover, I'm drunk. Drunk on Ella, on the night, on her kisses and touches. It's all I can think about as I walk across the park, the way I fell into kissing her, in a way I never have. I mean, sure, I have always liked kissing—who doesn't? But this was different. Like usually, even with Cassie, it feels like I'm kissing her and she's kissing me, and there's that sense of the two of us, separate. Not with Ella. With her it was like there was one kiss, made by one mouth, and the kiss was a space we both fell into, falling and falling into each other, and the air she breathed out was the same air I breathed in. I didn't ever want it to end, and even when we left this morning, as we moved away from each other my fingers held hers, letting go by degrees until my little finger was holding her little finger, and even in that smallest of touches, we were one. And nothing in my life ever felt so right.

I guess I should feel worse about Cassie, but after the double date it's hard to. I mean, maybe she was just jealous, but I didn't like that, being treated like that. Along the midway I see these guys at the ringtoss game or tossing softballs into bushel baskets, and they're determined to win the giant Goofy for their kids. So determined that they get pissed, red-faced, plunking down another twenty bucks on a stuffed toy that's worth about two bucks, slapping the money down and saying, Give me the damn things, and their kid is crying and doesn't' even want the giant Goofy anymore. That's how it felt with Cassie the last few days, like she doesn't even really want me, doesn't even like me all that much, but she's determined to have me, to have our night together at the Old Key West, to win.

I'm thinking this while I move through the park before it opens, watching all the maintenance people in their pastel T-shirts, some of them having snow cones for breakfast, some just coffee and cigarettes. There are a few families straggling around even though we aren't open yet, probably people there on some kind of special pass, or maybe just friends of someone. They look a little lost without a crowd to blend into, and sometimes it's easy to make fun of them with their matching mouse ears and cartoon maps and their desperate attention to character autograph lists. But this morning I'm in the mood to just let them be, even inside my head, because mornings in Florida are the best the place can be, before the day heats up, and because I can still feel Ella's fingers in my hair or cupping my face, and because there is every chance in the world that I'm in love with her.

I duck into the stand of scrub pines just past the end of the trolley track, on my way to Bernard's trailer. His keys are heavy, jingling in my hand as I walk, and I wonder how he did it, how he managed to steal or copy keys for thirty years without ever getting caught. Early this morning Ella and I curled up under a blanket together and looked at the list of keys, shaking our heads over and over. He had keys to Pleasure Island nightclub; to the planetarium controls in Epcot; to every store along Main Street, including ones that didn't exist anymore; to the Atlanta Braves lockers in Disney's Sports Complex; to the engine of the steamboat on the River Cruise. He could hijack the whole park if he wanted to.

"Maybe he will someday," I said. "Just take over, rename it Bernard Laurant World."

Ella smiled, then used one of the keys to lightly poke my thigh. "Nah," she said. "He would have made his move years ago. And obviously he's not a thief, the way he lives."

"Then why?" I said.

She thought a minute, twisting her pretty mouth. "I think he likes possibility."

"What do you mean?"

"Like, he can go anywhere. Nothing is closed to him. He doesn't have to go into those places, but he *can*. He can do anything he wants."

I nodded, but didn't say anything. We sat in the quiet, the keys flashing a little in the light.

Ella poked me again. "Nothing is closed to you, either," she said. I looked at her, wanting nothing more in the world than to believe that. I looked into her green eyes, at the way a faint blush rose across her cheeks, and I touched her mouth, and just then it felt like everything that had held me boxed in just fell away. If I could have *her*, if this perfect, oddball girl could find a way to love me, then anything seemed possible, and each moment would be a fistful of keys in a world of doors.

"Cinderella and Dale," I whispered. "That's going to be a pretty weird movie."

She nodded. "Weird in the best way. The story's full of surprises, so you have to stick around and see how it turns out."

"Will you?" I said. "Stick around?"

And even now—as I walk in the early light in the shadow of the castle, as the park slowly stirs itself to life—I can see her nodding, smiling as she leaned forward to kiss me again, whispering yes against my mouth.

. . .

There are two police cars parked outside Bernard's trailer, and a line of police tape runs from the stand of pines to the clothesline in his side yard to his front door. And it's not the tape they use inside the park if a bench breaks or someone throws up on a ride, the kind with the pink and blue Mickeys running across it. No, this is the real thing, yellow with black stripes, and all I can think is what Mark told us, that the security guys are actually real police. And then I think, *It's the keys.* I move closer to the trailer, to the female cop who stands against her squad car talking into the mike on her shoulder, and all that's running in my head is that somehow they know that Ella and me were in Walt's apartment last night, and that somehow it's Bernard's fault for giving us thirty years' worth of keys. I grip them in my hand, then reach down and slip them into the side pocket on my cargo shorts—carefully, so they don't jingle. And I have the impulse to just keep walking, but if he's in trouble because of us, I need to go in and narc on myself and get Bernard out of trouble, if I can.

I walk up to the woman officer, who ignores me while she looks over a clipboard, then talks to her shoulder in code. Like all the cops in the park, she's wearing the friendly looking white uniform with shorts. They always look like some obscure scout troop.

"May I help you?" she says.

"Well, yeah. Listen," I say. "I mean, what's going on?"

She looks up at me finally, her face sunburned, her hair pulled back into a severe ponytail. "Your name?"

"Luke," I tell her. "Luke Krause."

"And Luke, are you related to the deceased?"

I blink, look at her while something hardens deep in my stomach. "Deceased?"

She consults her clipboard. "One Bernard F. Laurant, park employee, white male, age fifty-seven."

"What do you mean?" I say as a blackness slowly closes around my vision.

"Son, maybe you should move along. The ambulance will be here any second."

"Ambulance . . ." For half a second I let myself think that ambulance must mean he's just sick, just needs to go to the hospital, and then I think how Bernard told me about the utilidors the first time we talked and how I would never actually see an ambulance in the park, and for half a strange second I have the impulse to wait around and see it just so I can tell him that I did.

I look again at her. "Bernard is dead?" I say.

She nods. "Coroner says natural causes. A little unusual given his age, so we're running it, anyway. Just routine."

Routine in the real world, I think, but I'm not really thinking it, because I find myself moving, just moving. *Away* is all my brain can say, over and over, and I run out along the rest of the trolley track, where it's just broken pieces of rail and rusting pieces cut off with a torch, and then around the back side of the lagoon, breaking through the trees and brush, and all I can hear is the sound of the pumps and the sound of my breathing, all ragged and choked and mingled together like it's not my breathing at all, and my hand keeps automatically slipping down to the keys in my side pocket, keeping them quiet as if they will still get us in trouble. And only one clear thought repeats in my brain—*He's dead, he's dead, he's dead.*

The first person to find me is Cassie, and she's not even looking. For half an hour I've been sitting under a tree at the back of the lagoon, trying to get my head around all of it, trying to remember the last time I saw Bernard when he was in costume, trying to remember the last thing he said to me. And then I wonder why it's so important to remember that way, and while I'm thinking about that I remember that he was going to teach me how to eat lunch without taking off my character head, a skill he said I would thank him for later, though I doubted it, wondering if *that* was the last thing he said to me. And then I keep circling around to thinking that this is silly, sitting here feeling so upset, and that I will just go over to Bernard's trailer and ask him, and then I remember all over again, like my brain keeps forgetting in three-minute cycles. My hands are shaking, and as I wipe my face with my T-shirt I hear a snap in the branches of the trees and look up, and there is Cassie.

"Hey," I say.

"This so much sucks," she says, and I nod.

"It does," I tell her. "I'm glad you're here."

"I mean, Mark can't find a stupid garden hose?" She gathers up her hair for a moment and fans herself with her hand. "We're in Florida, and there are, like, a million plants around this idiot place, and he can't find *one* hose?"

"Oh, yeah. Well . . ." I say, and let the sentence trail off.

Finally she notices me. "What's your problem?"

"Bernard. He's dead . . . he died."

She twists up her mouth. "Is that that guy on TV?"

I take a breath. "No, it's that guy who was my friend? I visited him at his trailer? Ate lunch with him? Foulfellow?"

"Oh, yeah . . . him." She moves toward me and sits on the pine needles beside me, where I'm slumped against the tree. "Well, I'm sorry," she says. "I know how close you were to him."

"I just don't get it. I never understood 'natural causes,' anyway. You don't just stop."

"Yes," she says, "you do. My granddad died at sixty, same thing. And then my grammy eight months after that. People *do* just stop, Luke." I look over at her, surprised to see actual tears in her eyes. Maybe the first real emotion from her.

I shake my head. "It sucks. I mean . . . it just sucks."

"And it's so pathetic, too," she says, wiping her eyes with her thumb. "The way he died. Alone in that little box, and you said he liked to drink. You said he was a nice guy; he deserved better." She keeps watching the side of my face.

"Maybe he died the way he lived, you know? Doing his own thing." I shrug, knowing as I say it how hollow it sounds.

"You think it was his thing to die like that? He just fell through the cracks, Luke." She leans toward me, and I try to pull away from her. I don't want this, and if I'm having any talk with Cassie, it should be about last night, about Ella, but right now everything just seems too big, too huge. Or maybe it's the opposite of that, maybe all my stuff seems too small compared to what happened to Bernard.

"Cassie, listen," I say, and draw a deep breath.

"No, you listen. I don't want that to happen to you. I don't want you to end up like that."

I look at her, surprised. "Me?"

"Yes, you. All this stuff about how you don't want that great job with your dad, how you want to just bum around for a while. Life is too short for that, Luke."

"Nice cliché. But I'd rather live by something a little more real."

"It's a cliché because it's true." She takes my hand, just holding it in her palm and looking at it as she talks. "Bernard ended up like that because he never made any other plans. He was just blown into the corner like a scrap of paper. It can happen."

"He chose it."

"You really believe that?" She looks at me.

I think about Bernard, *really* think about him, how in

some ways his proudest accomplishment was eating nachos without taking off his character head, about his trailer full of the yellowed past and used coffee filters. Maybe Ella was wrong about the keys, I think as I feel them pressing into my thigh. Maybe they weren't possibility to him, the chance to do anything he wanted, but more like keys to the prison—if he accumulated enough, or found the right one, he might find his way out. And of course, he never did, and never would.

"No," I say to Cassie, "I guess not."

She squeezes my hand, and without thinking, I squeeze back. "I know how people see me, as Miss Ambitious, or whatever. But you know what? I just want my life to be big, to be full. I want to really live it."

"Well, I do, too," I say.

"I know you do," she says, watching me. "But you don't do it by sitting back and letting life bring itself on. It might just bring a dinky trailer and a dead-end job. If you want a full life, you have to go *get* it."

I nod, thinking about this, wanting to argue with her, but not really finding a reason to. And the thought that letting life just happen might mean sitting around a crappy trailer forever waiting for something to come along . . . I feel my stomach pull into a hard knot. For a minute I can't breathe, and part of me just wants to jump up and run to wherever Ella is. But how can it be that my parents, Cassie, and the whole world are wrong, and only Ella and I have figured it out?

"Maybe you're right," I tell Cassie.

She turns my face to her and kisses me. "Yeah, I'm right. I can help you make your life big, Luke. I know how."

"Can we just talk more later?" I say to her.

She kisses me again, and I don't stop her. "Yes," she whispers. "We have a lot to talk about. And we have to work soon—are you coming with me?"

"I'm just going to sit here for a bit, okay? I don't want to face everyone just yet."

By the time I make it back to the dorm, the word is everywhere, and so are the rumors. Bernard was murdered. Bernard was murdered by the guy who plays Pinocchio. Bernard was a heroin addict. Bernard had a million dollars stashed in his trailer. It seems like any death is always accompanied by stories like that. Maybe the stories are just another set of keys—if people try enough, one will fit and somehow it will make sense. But it never does, not to me. Everyone wants to talk to me, and I see Amy leaning into Jesse, crying, but I don't have anything to say about any of it, and I just head to my room and lie on the bed, looking up at the ceiling. *I have to get out of here.* The words keep repeating inside me, crowding on top of each other like water filling my lungs, not letting me breathe. All I can think is that I have to get away, to get home . . . someplace safe where people aren't dying and I'm falling for a girl who lives a thousand miles away and my future slides out for miles ahead of me like a deep and bottomless hole, full of nothing. *Cassie's right*, I think, and then I say it out loud, to the ceiling.

"Yeah? What's she right about?" Ella says, just as I notice her walking into the room.

"Nothing," I say, wanting to pull her to me, but somehow there's a wall already between us, something off and awkward.

"Well, I think I agree with you there," she says, then pauses, her eyes filling with tears. "I'm so sorry about Bernard," she whispers. She sits on the edge of my bed, still wearing her Cinderella earrings, her hair up.

"Me, too," I say.

"This doesn't change anything," she says.

"No," I tell her, "it changes everything."

Her head snaps up like I've slapped her. She starts to say something and then doesn't, her eyes just searching my face.

I look away from her. "Ella, I like you, so much. I can't even say how much. But maybe we're just fooling ourselves. I mean, they settle the strike, and then what? What about us? We're seventeen years old. What are we supposed to do?"

She shakes her head. "Just be together. We should just be together."

"Just *poof*, like that? I mean, I fight the idea, but the truth is when I'm out of here, I have a really good job waiting for me, working right beside my dad and Ben instead of some idiot boss, and I'd be crazy not to—"

"Okay, am I talking to Luke or Cassie right now?" Her face flushes deep red.

"You don't have to like her, but Cassie's smart. Like I said, we leave here, and you go to Maine, or Cameroon maybe, and I'm a thousand miles away from you."

She nods, not saying anything, not looking at me, then stands and moves toward the door. She stops and turns back to me. "So," she says, "your answer is no."

I look at her. "No what? What do you mean?"

"No," she says, "you don't believe in magic."

By late that night my duffel bag and suitcase are both half-packed, sitting in the middle of the bed. Mark walks in looking exhausted and flops on his bed.

"You must be close to winning," I tell him.

"Yeah, another bloodletting or two and we'll have it."

I laugh. "Well, what's the hold up? I thought you would have won a week ago."

He nods. "Yeah, we almost did. We can't find a garden hose, we can't find a shovel, and we can't find PVC pipe. I don't even know what PVC pipe is."

"Yeah, you do. I told you."

He looks at me.

"You were drunk, and you asked me about the pipe, and I told you what it is. What I didn't tell you is *where* it is. And

Mark, the deal is it's underground. Go into any of those doors next to the restrooms that are marked AUTHORIZED PERSONNEL ONLY. That's us. Go in, and you'll be in a tunnel underground, and you will find PVC pipe, and you will find a garden hose."

"Really?"

"Really."

He sits up on the side of the bed and gives a little laugh. "Man. This means we win."

"That it does," I say, rolling up another pair of socks.

"Are you going somewhere?"

"I don't know. Maybe."

He watches me for half a minute. "I don't know what happened, but if you just go, you will break Ella's heart."

My own heart wobbles when he says her name. I shake my head. "I don't know what to do."

"Well, when I don't know what to do, I talk to my dad."

I almost laugh. I swear, Mark is so genuinely earnest that it's impossible to hate him for it. "Yeah," I say, "but your dad is a king. He's used to dispensing wise advice to his subjects. My dad, not so much."

"Actually, he *is* a king. He has this store THE TIRE KING. He bought it after he finished his career at Disney. He does these local commercials wearing a crown and shouting about prices on all-season radials."

"You're kidding me." I look at his face. "No, you aren't," I say.

• • •

After Mark leaves to tell Cassie the good news, I sit on my bed, my duffel bag full but only half-zipped, and an announcement comes over the PA to tell us that flags in the park will be at half-staff tomorrow and that Thursday will be declared Bernard Laurant Day. I think about Bernard, wishing that he could come back long enough to tell me one thing, to tell me if it was worth it, if he would do it again. Then I think about what Mark said, and I think, *What the hell*, and a minute later I'm at the end of the hall dialing the number for my dad's office. And even though it's eight o'clock at night, he picks up on the first ring.

"Hey, Sport," he says. "How's the chipmunk business these days?"

"Totally nuts," I say.

He laughs. "Wow, that is *really* bad. I see your joke-telling skills haven't changed."

There is an awkward pause, and I realize how long it's been since I talked to him, probably a month at least. And the last time I called him at work? I can't even remember.

"Dad?" I say. "I'm thinking of coming home. You know, so I can get started on my job and everything."

"Okay," he says, "let me talk to the kidnappers."

"What are you talking about?" I lean against the wall looking at all the old numbers scratched into the side of the pay phone.

"I've been expecting this phone call, Luke. But not *this*

phone call. I mean the one where you tell me you don't want the job, aren't coming home. I have eyes, son. I see your face when your brother and I are talking work."

"And what would you have said in that phone call?"

"I would have said you have to do what you have to do. My father told me the same thing."

"That's something you say when you're mad. Or disappointed." I move my fingertip over the scratches, tracing the numbers.

"Luke, I got married by a man in a tunic who tapped us on the shoulder with a plastic light saber when he finished. I haven't exactly always followed the narrow path."

"That's not an answer."

"Okay, sure I'm disappointed. I would like to have you here every day. I would like having my two boys with me all the time. But your life is not about me."

"Dad? What happened with all of that? The *Star Wars* stuff? I mean, are you just ashamed of it now?"

"Well, I was first in line for Episode Three, I can tell you that. Think of it this way . . . remember that stuffed dog you used to carry, Mr. Bones? With the bow tie?"

"Yeah."

"Well, you never carry him anymore. Are you ashamed of him?"

I nod. "I get it. Dad, thanks."

"Don't mention it. Oh, and Luke?" I can hear the smile in his voice. "Just use the Force, Luke."

I say my good-byes, hang up the phone, and walk back to my room to unpack. Just as I'm stuffing socks into the drawers, Mr. Tubbs comes on the intercom again to say there will be a special meeting of all temporary park employees at seven thirty the next morning. Then he tells us to have a Disney night. I look out the window at the castle, at our empty bench beneath the tree, wishing, wishing that I could make her just appear there. But she is gone, and the bench stays empty because I sent her away. And that's the thing about magic—once you stop believing, it goes away for good.

Ella

I keep thinking about the snow globe, wishing I hadn't given it to Luke to keep. Thinking about the tiny figures dancing inside. I keep turning it over in my head, watching as the snow collects on the top, then flipping it again so it swirls around the figures. It's funny how sometimes when things are turned upside down when you least expect it, everything gets so much more beautiful. And yet that's how it is with snow globes, why people buy them, or some people collect hundreds of them, lining them up on shelves in their houses, so that the insides of their houses are filled with hundreds of worlds. All ready to be turned over. All ready to be shaken up and then righted so that the snow swirls around inside, masking the scene for a few moments before it keeps swirling past, and instead of a blizzard, it's barely a sprinkling, then nothing. And it's in that final moment, as the snow settles back down to the bottom of the globe and the last few flakes drift lazily down, that you can really see everything clearly. Can see what has become of the figures inside. The ones locked in their dance, unable to change anything. It's then that you realize that's all there is, just the flip and the shake and the settle. And there's nothing beautiful in that at all.

"It's official," Amy says, walking back into our room. I don't answer her, haven't answered her all day. I actually haven't spoken to anyone since I talked to Luke. Well, except for Estrogen this morning when I told her I had food poisoning and I couldn't make it to the Princess Lunch. "Ella," Amy says. I feel the bed bump as she sits down and then the soft touch of her hand on my shoulder. "You can't do this," she says softly. "You can't just let go like this."

"What am I supposed to do?" I ask. Then I look at her. "What's official?"

"Mark and Cassie won the scavenger hunt," she says. "Big surprise."

"Yeah," I say. "Seems like everyone's full of surprises."

"You don't have to give me the details, just tell me enough so I know who to go beat the crap out of."

I laugh softly, then stop. "I think I'm going crazy," I say, closing my eyes.

"Then Robin Hood was right," she says. "Twice."

"Twice?" I ask, and sit up. She hands me a tissue and smiles.

"First about me and Jesse," she says, and her cheeks go pink.

"Really?" I ask. "What about the girl in Epcot?"

"It was an *interview*. Robin Hood conveniently forgot to tell me that the girl was actually Dr. Phoenix, the head of the horticulture division." She smiles and looks down at her hands. "I guess this isn't the best time to be telling you about this."

"No, tell me. I could use a little good news." I lean my head back against the wall and watch the side of her face.

"It's just amazing, you know?" she says, looking at me. I nod and smile slightly. I do know. "I mean, until about two weeks ago he was just Jesse, and then suddenly one day he was *Jesse*. And then I couldn't stop thinking about him, looking at him. It was as if the whole world just collapsed down into a single point. Does this make any sense?" I nod again, trying to stay focused on Amy and Jesse, but it's hard.

"What's the deal with the interview at Epcot?" I ask.

"Well, here's the thing," Amy says, looking back down at her hands. "He got offered this internship here for the fall."

"And you're supposed to go back home for school."

"Yeah," she says so softly it's almost like she breathed it instead of spoke it. "I don't know what to do."

"What does Jesse say?" I ask.

"He wants me to stay, and thinks I can land an internship,

too. But he said it was up to me. Told me we'd do the long-distance thing."

"Yuck," I say, but part of me thinks that even long-distance would be better than this. At least with long-distance, there's someone at the other end of the rope tugging gently every once in a while, so you know he's still there. With this it's like the rope got cut and I'm slowly falling backward into thin air.

"I guess we have some time to figure it out. I mean, it's not like we have to make up our minds right now," she says, but the catch in her voice tells me she wants something more solid than *maybe* and *later* to stand on. "So, about you," she says, turning toward me. "Tell me." I close my eyes.

"There's nothing to tell," I say, but when I say it out loud, I hate the words. Hear them repeating inside my head, but instead of getting softer like an echo, they get louder until all I can hear is *nothing* again and again. And I wonder how it is that nothing can make you feel like this.

"It's the best cure," Robin Hood says, passing a glass of orange juice in my direction.

"What's in it?" I ask. I sniff the juice, trying to smell something other than citrus.

"Orange juice," he says slowly, like I'm not quite there, and to tell the truth, I'm not. Amy dragged me out, saying I had to eat something, that I couldn't just hide away for the rest of the summer.

"Orange juice and what else?" I ask, tilting my head at him.

"Look, Ella, vitamin C is one of the best cures for a broken heart."

"I thought that was beer."

"That, too," he says, forking another triangle of pancakes into his mouth. "But maple syrup and beer do not mix. Trust me on this one." I take a tiny sip, not quite trusting him. "Ye of little faith." He smiles at me, then continues. "So do you want me to kick his ass?" he asks. I can't help but smile at him. Solidarity through vulgarity. We both look over at where Cassie is sitting with an empty chair beside her. "He's not worth it. I mean, Cassie is smokin' for sure."

"Is this you trying to cheer me up?" I ask, taking another drink of the juice. Robin Hood puts his fork down and looks at me.

"You ready for your laundry payment?" he asks.

"I thought Mark did that for you." I pick up my toast and take a tiny bite of it.

"He half did it."

"So, what's the rest of it?" I ask. I look over again at the empty chair, then back at Robin Hood, feeling the toast stick at the back of my throat.

"It's simple, Princess. You have to jump back in the water. Stop standing on the dock and watching." He bites into a piece of bacon. "I mean that metaphorically," he says.

"I got that." I take another sip of orange juice.

"Look, you got dunked this time, but next time it'll be different," he says. He shoves the rest of the piece of bacon into his mouth and stands up. He nods once and walks over to dump his tray.

"Next time," I say softly, standing up to throw away the rest of my breakfast. I keep repeating it to myself, trying to make it drown out the echoes already filling my head. But instead of muting each other, they get all mixed up. *Next time nothing. Nothing next time.* Then it's quiet.

It's funny, really, all the ways we tell ourselves every day that things are going to be okay. That things are going to get better, or that things can't possibly get any worse. We all have these elaborate mechanisms to take care of our disappointments, our sadness, our pain. We build these walls around ourselves, placing bricks between us and everyone else, telling ourselves that we're just protecting ourselves, just staying safe. Sometimes the bricks are easy to see, hard things that you bump up against when you try to touch someone. Sometimes they're subtle. A slight turn of the head, a fast good-bye, a faraway look in the eyes. Sometimes I wonder why Disney never took to Rapunzel, why they never tried to take that story and put it on lunch boxes and in video stores and on pink sweatshirts. Maybe it's that some fairy tales don't need to be computer animated. Maybe Randy Newman doesn't need to sing their songs. Maybe some fairy tales don't even really need to be told, because they live inside of us, scaring us with their witches and their evil spells, making us wonder if maybe this time the prince won't come in time, the princess won't wake up, and maybe for once there won't be any happily ever after. Maybe some fairy tales are just too scary to even think about.

"There's a meeting," Amy says, stepping into the tent, where I am busy trying to push my pink dress into the laundry bag. An overzealous mother managed to knock a whole pitcher of red punch into my lap during the Princess Brunch.

"When?" I ask, blotting at the red stain that somehow made its way through the seventeen layers of tulle and onto my shorts.

"Now. Mr. Tubbs told me to come get you and Mark. Most everyone else is already in the conference room." I raise my eyebrow at her, but she just shrugs. "They didn't say what it was about."

"Do you think they . . ." I don't even bother finishing my question. The thought of leaving here now makes me panic in about fifty different ways. Amy walks over to the table at the back of the tent and pulls three water bottles out of the cooler.

"Here," she says, handing me one of them. "We'll wait outside." I don't have a chance to ask who "we" is before she walks out, letting the flap shut behind her. I give up on the stain on my shorts and reach into my backpack for my other pair before remembering that I didn't replace the spare ones last night after a little boy threw popcorn and blue Gatorade all over me after the Electrical Parade. I pull my pack over my shoulders and walk outside, lifting my hand to shield my eyes. Amy and Jesse don't even look up until I am almost on top of them.

"Ella," Jesse says.

"Jesse." I nod at him and smile, making him smile back at me. We start walking toward the conference center. Amy and Jesse holding hands. Me holding my water bottle.

"As I was saying . . ." Estrogen begins, but the noise in the room is too loud to hear the rest of what she is trying to say. A loud squeal of the microphone as she taps it makes everyone quiet down a bit. "We are happy to announce that as of ten o'clock this morning, union representatives and management have reached an agreement . . ."

"Only because the maintenance workers threatened to walk," Robin Hood says, leaning back in his chair.

"Garbage could bring this place to its knees," Amy says, making me look over to where Luke is sitting with Cassie, but he isn't paying attention to her or to us; instead, he's working on something, bending it back and forth in his fingers. Cassie looks up at me and smiles, but only with her mouth.

"I guess that's it," Robin Hood says, giving Anna a squeeze. "Fun while it lasted."

"Again, we want to thank all of you for your efforts this summer," Estrogen says. "You are welcome to stay on for the remainder of the week until you get your plans firmed up, but we would like to have the hotel back online by Monday."

"Don't let the door hit you in the ass on the way out," Robin Hood says. Around me I hear people already making plans. Cell phones are taken from pockets and packs, and suddenly people are all talking into them and not to each other. Already away from here. Already gone.

"So you're staying," I say, dropping bottles of shampoo and conditioner into Ziplocs before pushing them into my duffel bag. Mickey smiles up at me from everything. New back-pack, new sweatshirt, new makeup bag. All courtesy of Disney. "Thank you for a job well done," the notes all said.

"I am," Amy says. "Dr. Phoenix gave us the name of one of the professors who's going on sabbatical this fall. She said he might need a house sitter."

"What did your parents say?" I ask.

"They were all freaked-out at first, but then I told them I might be working in the digital animation studio as an intern, and that calmed them right down." She smiles at me, and I can't help but smile back. "Listen, I told Jesse I'd meet him at three to go over to the house." She turns her wrist to look at her watch. Snow White's arms twist in impossible directions as they wind their way around the face. "Will you be here when I get back? It should only take an hour."

I shake my head. "My bus is at four. Robin Hood is giving me a ride to the station."

"Back to Aunt Sara's?" she asks.

"Just for a couple of weeks."

"Then it's up to Vermont?"

"I guess," I say, but somehow it doesn't seem that exciting anymore. "I almost forgot." I reach into my pocket for a card and hand it to Amy. "Mark's card. He told me to give one to you."

She holds it up and reads aloud: "Assistant to the Manager of Special Productions." She looks up at me. "What does that mean?"

I shrug. "They just told him that he was the best Prince Charming they'd ever had, and they didn't want him to get away. He seemed really excited. He also said Luke had been by and gave him something, but he wouldn't tell me what." Just saying Luke's name makes it hard to breathe. I look down at my duffel and pull at the zippers, closing it tight.

"Well, I have something for you," Amy says, reaching into the front pocket of her backpack. She pulls out two index cards and hands them to me. "These are the last ones. I gave back all the others when I figured them out." I flip the first one over, seeing my own handwriting slanted down to the right, uneven letters marching downhill. "It's weird that they'd both be the same," she says. "Exactly the same." I nod, reading the second card. "I want." Just two words, the same two I printed on my secret card. But these are smaller and off to the left. Lots of room for the rest. I look up at Amy, and she shrugs. "I have something else for you, but it's not from me." She reaches behind her bag and pulls out a bundle of tissue paper and hands it to me. I know what it is before I even fold my fingers around it. "He left it here this morning. Said you'd understand." I nod and place the bundle on my bed before hugging her.

"I'll call you," I say into her hair.

"You better," she says, and then she pulls back and looks at me.

"What?" I ask.

"Jesse's right," she says. "You do look like her."

"Like who?" I ask, but she just shrugs and squeezes my arm. She smiles again briefly before walking to the door. A quick wave and she's gone. I walk over toward the bed, past the bundle leaning against my pillow and to the window. I start packing again, until the sound of a loud muffler makes me look down into the parking lot. An orange car makes a wide arc before stopping in front of the entrance. I hurry to push the rest of my things into my backpack, sliding the cards into my visitor's guidebook. Also courtesy of the Disney Family. I lift the bundle on my pillow and shift the paper down until I can see the glass top. I turn it over and shake it until all of the snow collects on the top, then flip it, pulling the paper down farther so I can watch it swirl. I hear footsteps walking toward me down the hall, then pausing in the doorway. I keep watching the globe, trying to see in between the flakes. Trying to catch a glimpse of the dancers. Cinderella appears, her blond hair caught up in a white band, her arms outstretched holding the prince's hands. But not like any prince I've ever seen. Instead of Prince Charming, she's dancing with something much furrier. Something resembling a tiny chipmunk.

"Jesse *is* right," a voice says from the doorway. I look up to see Luke standing there, his keys dangling from his hand. "You do," he says.

"I do what?" I ask, tilting my head at him.

"You look like her. Just like Cinderella."

Luke

"I have to say," Ella says to me, "this is one of the ugliest cars I have ever seen."

I nod and glance over at her through my sunglasses, not taking my eyes off the road for too long. The traffic is heavy this time of year. "Thanks," I tell her, and squeeze her hand, which rests inside mine on the seat between us.

"Why orange?" she says. Her own sunglasses are made for little kids, bright green with smiling Mickeys perched over the corners.

"Well, there were important aesthetic considerations to think about," I say as I head north down a two-lane black-top. "I mean, before I started to paint, I had to think about color organically, deciding exactly what shade the perfect 1993 Subaru would be in a perfect world, and so—"

"You are so full of it," she says. "And wait, *you* painted it? You know how to do all that auto shop stuff?" She absently turns over the snow globe in her lap, making the snow move around inside.

"I painted it with spray cans I bought at Wal-Mart," I tell her, and she laughs. My dad has always been the work-for-what-you-get type, and after a summer of mowing every lawn in town, this car was the best I could do. "You know how many cans it took? *Two hundred.*"

"So orange was the color of the perfect idea of the perfect Subaru, huh?"

I nod. "Absolutely. And orange was on sale."

She laughs again and slips over closer to me, holding my arm in her hands, resting her head against my shoulder. The radio plays hits from the '70s and '80s while the air-conditioning blows the salt smell of the ocean through the car. She turns her face toward me long enough to kiss my shoulder. "I like you," she whispers. I smile, then reach up to stroke her hair.

"I like you, too," I say.

"I just have one question," she says, still whispering. "How did you replace Prince Charming with Dale?"

"Well, Ella, you know Mark was never really right for you, and so I just waited patiently, and after a time—"

She smacks my thigh. "No, goofball, how did you replace him in *this*?" She holds up the globe and shakes it, then turns the key and watches Cinderella and Dale dance around in the snow. She holds it right up to her eyes so that, she says, they look life-size.

"The usual hard work and perseverance," I say. "I had to run the stuff through a coffee filter to save the snow, then break off the Prince without breaking the glass, then cover the base of the Prince with a Dale pencil topper."

"Wow."

"I spilled some of the liquid, so then I had to find out the right mixture of water and glycerin, *then* find the glycerin, and then put it all back together."

"You're amazing," she says.

I shrug. "I just thought you would like it."

"I love it. One more question?"

"One?" I say. "We have lots of time ahead of us. You'd better have thousands of questions."

"One for now? Amy said you gave something to Mark?"

"Yeah, I gave him the snapped-off Prince Charming . . ." I look at her. "I'm *kidding*. I gave him Bernard's keys."

She nods. "That seems right. Man, he must love you. That's like Christmas and birthday in one shot."

"Unless he gives them back. Rules are rules if you're him, I think."

She moves her thumb across the palm of my hand. "I know, but I don't think he will. I think he will think no one else in the world can be trusted with those keys."

"In that case, I think he's right."

Ella opens a Disney bottled water and tips some into my

mouth before drinking some herself. "I don't want to spoil the morning," she says, "but what about Cassie?"

"What about her?" I shrug. "She won the contest. Right now I suspect she's at the Old Key West lounging by the pool, checking out the lifeguards. She's not much of one for altering her plans."

"You scared me the last few days," she says, her voice quieter. I slow down and look at her, watch her fingers wind the key again so that again, we hear "When You Wish Upon a Star" while the snow swirls in a slow circle.

"Scared you how?"

"I thought you'd gone over to the dark side," she says, and smiles a little. Then the smile fades and she looks out the window. "I can't lose somebody else," she whispers.

I squeeze her hand. "I can't go over to the dark side," I tell her. "I'm Luke Skywalker. It would screw up the whole story."

She nods. "So Cassie went to the hotel by herself?"

"Can you think of anyone else she'd rather be with?"

She shakes her head, then pulls something from the back pocket of her shorts. She holds up a pair of wrinkled index cards. "Remember these?"

"Amy the All-Powerful," I say. "Why do you have them?"

"Well, one is mine." She holds it up so I can read it: "I want."

"Hey, wait a second," I say. I look again at the card, but it's not my handwriting. "You won't believe—"

"And the other one she can't figure out. The weird thing is, it says the same as mine."

She holds it up, and this time I do recognize my own handwriting. Just then it starts raining those fat Florida raindrops that hit the windshield with a splat. I pull off my sunglasses and look at Ella, and she does the same. "That's my card," I tell her.

She smiles. "I was kinda hoping," she says. She props them both up on top of the dash, just under the windshield, side by side. "I got rushed and dropped it in. But probably it was my brain being smarter than me. I mean, I don't know what I want. But I know I do want *something*, you know?"

"Yeah, it's hard to be specific."

"What do you want, Luke?" She really looks at me, her green eyes flecked with copper. The radio station fades out, and we ride to the rhythm of the wipers. When I check the rearview, I notice the spires of Cinderella's castle still barely visible behind us.

"Everything," I say, and look at her again.

"Yep. Not very specific."

"I didn't finish," I tell her. "Everything . . . and you. And if I can have you right here beside me, I think the everything might not matter so much."

She blushes and smiles, reaches up to touch my hair. She opens her window a little to let in the smell of the rain, and our index cards flutter on the dash.

"Ask me what I want," she says.

I clear my throat. "Ella," I say, "what do you want?"

She smiles. "You, right here beside me." She squeezes my hand, leans into me. "And a hamburger." She smiles big.

"Nice. Are those two ranked in any particular order?"

"Oh, you are definitely first. The hamburger is merely a close second." She kisses the side of my face. "And I mean it. All that crappy food we had? I want a *real* burger, on a sourdough roll, with real tomato. And fries."

"I know just the place. They have the best burgers in the world, I think. Wanna go?"

"Sure. Where is it?"

"Memphis," I tell her, and cut my eyes at her. "That's in Tennessee."

She laughs. "Well, I might need some Junior Mints or something to tide me over, since it's like . . . how far away? Two days?"

"Yeah, if we take our time."

She nods. "Let's do that."

I nearly miss the next exit ramp heading west. As we turn, I glance up into the rearview and try to see the fiberglass castle disappear behind us. By now the rain has stopped, and sunlight fills the car. Ella leans as we turn, one arm holding on to me, the other holding up the glass snow globe near her eyes again as the music plays. She tips it slightly so that all of the snow settles to one side of the globe. For that moment the two of them, Dale and Cinderella, dance in the bright sparkle of water, all the snow gone, nothing clouding their vision.

Turn the page for a sneak peek at
Brad Barkley and Heather Hepler's next book

CHAPTER ONE

Chloe

I THINK THERE are these lies that we tell each other. Like when you go to the dentist and he asks if you floss every day and you tell him yes, even though you know it's not true and he knows it's not true. And, somehow it's just understood or even expected because he knows that you know all the reasons why you should floss, and you know he knows all the reasons why you don't. Or like the lie you tell your father when he asks how your day was, and you say fine or nothing when really Branda, the girl who sits in front of you in English, told you that your hands feel like a dead person's because they're so cold all the time. And when she said it everyone laughed, and you had to pretend to laugh, too, because if you didn't, it wouldn't ever stop and suddenly you'd be known as the girl-with-hands-that-feel-like-a-dead-person's, even though you know it can't be true because you've *felt* a dead person's hands, and they didn't feel like that at all.

The bins at the Wild Oats Market are all arranged by category. All the nuts are together, and the dried cherries are between the papaya spears and banana chips. And all the decaf coffees are at the end of the row marked with green signs so no one accidentally gets decaf when they thought they were getting regular. The candies are all along one wall, like some cubist painting made out of gummy worms and candy LEGO blocks and chocolate-covered almonds and sour watermelon balls. I'm trying to decide between the red licorice swirls and the black licorice swirls and watching as a woman beside me keeps dipping scoop after scoop of English toffee pieces into a plastic bag.

"I really don't need this," she says, letting the plastic door close on the top of the bin. The bag is so heavy that it makes her fingers white where she's holding it. She twirls it twice, letting the top close in on itself before fastening it with a green twist-tie. "I just can't help myself." She looks up at me and smiles, and I realize that she's talking to me, which is funny because no one ever talks to me, except to ask me to pass something or find something or do something. I smile with my lips closed. The smile that I've been perfecting, that says *that's amusing* or *that's nice* or *isn't that interesting*. And I think that's it, she is going to turn and weigh her toffee and walk over to her cart and put the bag in next to her taro chips and her bottles of organic lemonade. But she doesn't.

Instead she tilts her head at me and asks, "Aren't you one of Ellie's daughters?" And just like that, the last eleven months of holding my breath don't count for anything.

I nod, and I know what's coming next. The soft look and the cluck of the tongue and the two words that I've come to hate—I'm sorry. But then instead of closing her eyes, as if my pain is too much to bear, she smiles. "I thought I recognized you," she says. "I haven't seen her in class in so long. How is she?" I keep looking at her yellow clogs. I can hear my father's voice a couple of rows over, having both sides of a conversation about cashew butter and almond butter.

"She's fine," I say, because it seems like the thing I'm supposed to say. The expected lie, the nod when my dentist asks if I floss every day. I glance up and smile, then look her right in the eye, because that's what I also know is expected. You have to make them believe it. It's not that hard to lie to her, because I guess it's not really a lie. She *might* be fine. I just don't know. My father's voice gets louder and I can hear the thunk of my sister's boots. Slow and rhythmic, like a heatbeat.

"Well, tell her to come back. We miss her." I nod again and turn back to the candy bins, even though now the thought of eating makes me feel sick. "Yoga just isn't as much fun without her there." I don't look at her as she loads her cart and makes a slow three-point turn to head toward the bakery section and the checkout. I can hear the sound of Micah's boots now, too, the soft squeak of rubber on linoleum as he walks slowly behind my father. I lean forward and grip the plastic tongs with one hand, stretching the coiled cord that keeps them attached to the bin.

"Come on, slowpoke," my father says to me as they make the turn around the loose teas and into the candy aisle. I pinch half a dozen red swirls and drop them into my bag, then let the top of the bin drop closed. But the noise it makes is loud, too loud. I turn, running my fingers along the top of the bag, feeling the rows of plastic, each fitting into another, sealing the bag closed.

Our apartment takes up the whole top floor of our building. My bedroom is at the front, overlooking the street, just past the kitchen on the left. My father says that my room used to be the servant quarters when this building was filled with the families of wealthy businessmen, living off the shipping industry. It's separated from the rest of the bedrooms, which are all along the back of the apartment, overlooking the garden tucked behind our building, hidden from the street. We got to pick our rooms in order of our age, so Shana went first. I thought for sure she'd want my room, with its window seat and sloped ceiling, but she chose the big room in the back corner with the built-in bookcase. I went next. I was going to take the room that Micah has now, but my father thought that maybe Micah would be afraid all by himself on the other side of the apartment. Of course that was before we'd met him.

The move to Portland was my father's idea. We used to live in an old cape on the other side of Brunswick, right near the ocean. In the summer, we would take our old camp blankets and sandwiches wrapped in waxed paper to the beach for dinner. We'd walk the length of it—exactly a mile each way—every night, my mother and father holding hands and Shana and me splashing through the wet sand, filling our pockets with bits of sea glass and empty mussel shells. When it got dark, we'd walk back home, our flip-flops covered in sand and seaweed, our hands full of stones and seagull feathers. Our pockets too full to hold anything more. Now, there are no more walks. We eat at the kitchen counter, in shifts, dipping bowls of soup or chili from the Crock-Pot set on low at the back of the counter. Shana and I keep an eye on Micah, making sure he eats, fixing him sandwiches and milk to go with his dinner.

I remember in the fall, with the leaves turning orange and gold, we used to walk down to the end of the driveway, where we'd catch the school bus to St. Joe's. Shana and I sat together when we were little, pressed close for warmth, in the seat just behind the driver. Once she was in sixth grade and I was in fifth, she stopped sitting with me every day, preferring most days to be with her friends in the back of the bus, where they would make folded paper flowers, capable of predicting your future. These days we just walk the three blocks over to the City School on Exchange Street. We used to take turns walking Micah to day care, making sure he had his mittens and his lunch, holding his hand when we crossed the street. That was back when our apartment was filled with the smell of turpentine and freshly baked brownies. Now only I walk with Micah every day, making my steps small to match his. Even though she never looks back, I always watch Shana as she walks in front of us, her black scarf whipping across her back in the wind. I keep looking forward, holding Micah's mittened hand tightly in mine as my sister disappears around the corner.

"Chloe, can you please come help put the groceries away?" my father calls from the kitchen. The bed creaks as I stand up. It does that only when I stand up, never when I sit down. Exactly the opposite of what you would expect. My father is standing in the middle of the kitchen on a tiny island of tile surrounded by the sea of double-bagged groceries that we carried up the stairs from the car. We usually bag the groceries ourselves. We make two of them heavy, for my father to carry, filled with half gallons of milk and glass jars of salsa and spaghetti sauce and pickled beets. Four bags are lighter—two for Shana and two for me. Lemons and bananas and mango apricot yogurt and whole wheat fig bars. The last two are for Micah. The lightest ones, macaroni and bread and spinach and black bean chips. It's like the Goldilocks method of bagging groceries. We put them away in silence. Most everything is done in silence here. The quiet has become so normal that it sometimes startles me when I hear the honk of a horn from the street below or the call of a raven flying overhead.

From the kitchen, you can see into the living room. For a long time we didn't own a television, but got a small one finally because Micah was used to it, liked watching it. In the *dyet dom*, where they stored all the orphans, they used either television or a shot of aminazine to keep them quiet. I guess Micah was lucky he got the TV.

"Hey, little guy," my father says. He sounds tired. Micah walks into the kitchen, balancing a plate on the top of his glass. He steps over the mound of empty plastic bags and toward the sink. He might have made it if it weren't for the jar of pickles partly hidden under the mound. I put my hands out instinctively as he stumbles. The plate tips at an impossible angle, sliding from its perch before crashing to the floor. At once Micah is on his knees, fumbling with the shards of pottery still spinning away from him on the tile.

"It's okay," I say, putting my hand on Micah's back. He shrinks under it, pulling away from my touch, as if from something unbearably hot. I see the splash of tears on the floor as his hands scramble at the sharp edges of the broken plate.

"Micah," my father says, softly, kneeling beside him on the floor. "It's okay." A slash of red appears on Micah's hand as one of the pieces catches him between his thumb and forefinger. "Micah, please," my father says, folding his large hands around Micah's tiny ones. They stay like that for several moments before I help Micah stand. "Let's get you cleaned up," I say, leading Micah to the sink. He looks up at me, his eyes still wet with tears.

"It's okay," I whisper. And I wish just by saying it, I could make it so.

I always leave my window open a bit while I sleep. The cold air drifts in, smelling of the ocean and smoke. I can hear the crunch of tires as cars pick their way over the icy cobblestones in the street below, and if I listen closely I can make out the clang of the harbor buoy, echoing off the buildings. Right now I hear a rustling past my door. My father is doing his nightly rounds. He checks on me first, then Shana, and last Micah. I wait, listening to the fading whispers from his slippers and creaks of the wood floor. I pull on my robe, my father's old flannel one, which I rescued from the Salvation Army bag. Meant to hang just past the knees, it puddles on the floor around my feet as I walk down the hall. I hear the door to my mother's studio open and close, then another noise. This one so soft that I might not hear it at all if I didn't know to listen.

Shana is by the door, holding her boots in one hand, twisting her dark scarf around her neck with the other. She bends down to pull on her boots, lifting one foot at a time, balancing carefully as she pulls the laces tight.

"Where are you going?" I ask, careful to whisper.

"Out," she says without looking at me. And really, it's

hard for me to look at her when she's all made up like that, her face so white and so black, both. I pull at the collar of my robe, feeling the chill of the apartment settle around me.

"What about Dad?" I ask.

"You know he never knows," she says, finally meeting my gaze, and she's right. Each night, after making sure the doors are locked and we are all tucked in our beds, he goes in there. I've heard him murmuring to himself, his voice softly rumbling as he walks through the room. I've pressed my ear against the door, listening to the clink of wood against glass as he fingers her brushes clustered in empty Mason jars and orphan coffee mugs. I've heard him crying quietly, saying her name over and over into the empty room.

"Take me with you," I say to Shana. *Take me to wherever you go every night. Take me to where there is noise and light and laughter. Take me to where you forget.*

"I can't," she says, so softly that I barely hear more than a breath of words. And again I know she's right. To take me would be to take what she is trying to escape. She fingers her bracelets, all leather and rubber, except one. The one that mirrors mine and seems oddly out of place. She pushes her hair out of her face, tucking it behind her ears. Both of us used to have hair the color of honey, shimmering in the sunlight. Hers is dyed black, stark against her pale skin. Not the soft black of a velvety cat or the endless black of a night sky. Her hair is flat and featureless, so dark that it seems that if you fell into it, you would be lost forever.

Chloe

We both hear a soft whimper in the dark, Micah having another of his dreams. "I'll be back," she says, reaching her hand toward mine. For a moment, as she touches my wrist, I can almost remember how it used to be. How my mother would pull us tight against her at night to tell us another of her stories filled with dragons and magic and wishes come true. How she would kiss the tops of our heads before tucking us into bed. "My little bookends," she would whisper. She was always between us, holding us together. Now, she is always between us, keeping us apart. "Go back to bed," Shana says, twisting the doorknob. "I'll see you in the morning." The air from the hall is cold on my face. She pulls the door behind her shut with a click.

I hear it again. A whimper from down the hall. My father turns over on the couch in the studio. He is listening, too. He'll stay there all night, curled on the dusty sofa. My mother's old barn coat pulled over him for warmth. In the morning, he will greet us at breakfast, his whiskers and hair smelling of turpentine and mold. Smells that will mix with the scent of cinnamon and maple syrup. It is as if we all lead night lives, separate from the people we are in the light.

I listen for another moment, hearing only the creak of the building settling in on itself as it pulls in from the cold. I float between remembering and forgetting. Halfway between my father and Shana. Some days I feel like I am going to drown in my memories, that I am going to be pulled under by my mother's tide, which tugs at all of us. Other nights, like tonight, I worry that I will forget. That slowly my memories will crack and fade, like paintings left out in the sun.

I walk down the hall to the silence of my bedroom and look at the jars of sea glass lined up on my windowsill, slowly winking in the light from the street below. A blue and green and amber mosaic pieced together over the years, one bit at a time. It became a game in my family to see if we could find a piece of red sea glass, so rare as to be almost a legend. My mother swore one of us would find it someday, when we least expected it. I shove my hands into the pockets of my robe, warming them in the depths of the flannel. I feel something in one of them, something flat and hard. Something rubbed smooth by the sand until its rough edges have disappeared. I take off my robe and hang it on the door without taking the bit of glass from my pocket. As I climb into bed and pull my quilt up to my chin, I tell myself it is probably just a normal piece of sea glass. One that I had forgotten was there. Probably just an oval of green or blue. I tell myself that maybe in the morning it will be gone, just a flutter of a dream that I had. What I don't tell myself is what might be true. That the bit of glass in the pocket of my robe might be red. Because in my family things like that aren't allowed to happen. In my family if you believe in wishes or dreams or magic, you might just end up like her.

Chloe